Praise for

The Tin Snail

"A captivating book for young people of all ages."
—T. E. Carhart, bestselling author of
The Piano Shop on the Left Bank

"Charming." —*The Guardian* (UK)

"A thoroughly engaging read." —*The Spectator* (UK)

"A delightful book." —Historical Novel Society

"Feel-good, funny, romping, filmic adventure."
—*The Sunday Times* (London)

"A fantastic family read." —*Mr. Ripley's Enchanted Books*

"Unusual and delightful." —*Parents in Touch*

"Refreshingly different and very engaging." —*Reading Zone*

"I loved this delightful novel. It's intended for middle grade readers but people of all ages will love it." —*The Bookbag*

the TiN SNAiL

Cameron McAllister

Illustrated by Sam Usher

Delacorte Press

Text copyright © 2014 by Cameron McAllister
Jacket and interior illustrations copyright © 2014 by Sam Usher

All rights reserved. Published in the United States by Delacorte Press, an imprint of Random House Children's Books, a division of Penguin Random House LLC, New York. Originally published in hardcover by Random House Children's Publishers UK, London, in 2014. This edition published by arrangement with Random House Children's Publishers UK, a division of Penguin Random House Ltd.

Delacorte Press is a registered trademark and the colophon is a trademark of Penguin Random House LLC.

Visit us on the Web! randomhousekids.com

Educators and librarians, for a variety of teaching tools, visit us at RHTeachersLibrarians.com

Library of Congress Cataloging-in-Publication Data
McAllister, Cameron.
The Tin Snail / Cameron McAllister ; illustrated by Sam Usher. — First American edition.
    pages cm
"Originally published . . . by Random House Children's Publishers UK, London, in 2014."
Based on the true story of the Citroen 2CV car.
Summary: "A thirteen-year-old French boy tries to save his father's job by inventing a special kind of car, but it isn't easy—especially when the Nazis are planning to steal his design"—Provided by publisher.
ISBN 978-0-553-53638-6 (hc) — ISBN 978-0-553-53640-9 (lib. bdg.)
ISBN 978-0-553-53641-6 (pbk) — ISBN 978-0-553-53639-3 (ebook)
[1. Automobiles—Design and construction—Fiction. 2. Fathers and sons—Fiction. 3. Italians—France—Fiction. 4. France—History—German occupation, 1940–1945—Fiction. 5. World War, 1939–1945—Underground movements—France—Fiction.] I. Usher, Sam (Illustrator), illustrator. II. Title.
PZ7.1.M4Ti 2016
[Fic]—dc23
2014048814

The text of this book is set in 12-point Goudy.
Jacket design by Sarah Hokanson
Interior design by Stephanie Moss

Printed in the United States of America
10 9 8 7 6 5 4 3 2 1
First American Edition

Random House Children's Books supports the First Amendment and celebrates the right to read.

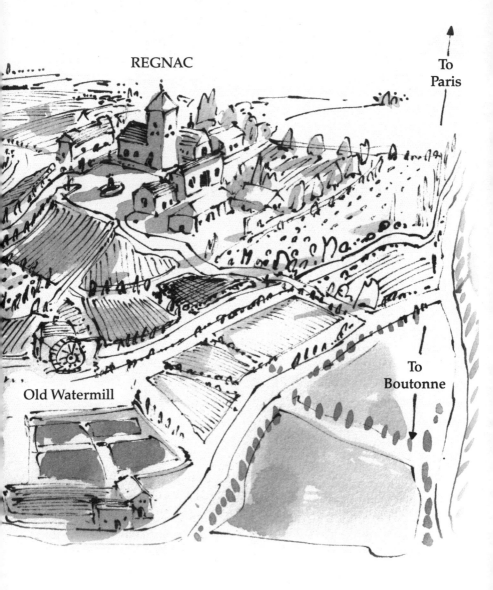

REGNAC

To
Paris

To
Boutonne

Old Watermill

the
TiN SNAiL

1 Nine Spoonfuls of Sugar

I watched the short, tanned figure of my father pour an eighth teaspoon of sugar into his coffee. This might sound odd—and it was—but there are two things you need to know about my father right from the start.

The first is that his name was Luca Fabrizzi, which, if you haven't guessed, is Italian (and, as everyone knows, Italians love their coffee). The second is that there was one thing Papa loved even more than coffee, and that was sugar. He wasn't too fussed what form it took—though he was particularly partial to pains au chocolat and the sticky fruit fondants created in the pâtisserie across the road from his workshop. But his favorite treat of all was strong, sweet coffee—preferably with enough sugar in it to prop up a teaspoon.

It was the same every morning. An hour before school,

sometimes more, we would come to the Café Petit Chemin de Fer ("the Little Railway Café"), tucked away behind the old railway line that divided my father's workshop from the row of shabby little shops across the street. Looming high above was the factory where my father's latest designs were turned into reality—a vast structure with arched windows like a cathedral that looked out over the river Seine.

Why were we living in Paris? Because my father and mother, Julietta, had run away from home together when they were seventeen. Papa had originally wanted to be an artist and had come to Paris to make his fortune . . . but more on that later.

Inside the café, my father would always order an espresso—a miniature cup, usually stained around the edge, with a double shot of thick, oily coffee that looked like tar. He insisted he needed it to wake him up. The spoonfuls of sugar he loaded into it? Well, that was for inspiration. Only then could the magical ideas take shape.

I would tuck into a large bowl of hot chocolate. Not the powdered sort, either. The café owner, a large woman with big hips whom Papa had once described as "voluptuous," always flaked real dark chocolate into the milk. I loved sipping from the edge of the bowl, the swathes of creamy steam wafting around my face.

On this particular day, a bone-numbing winter's morning toward the end of 1937, a few months after my twelfth birthday, I watched, fascinated, as my father's teaspoon began its journey back to the bowl for the ninth time. Even by his standards this had to be a spoonful too far. Sure enough, as the sugar was heaped into his cup, the thick black tar started to brim over the edge.

"Papa," I hissed.

My father looked over, frowning, and quickly saw the mess. "Blast!" He snatched paper napkins from the little metal dispenser and began furiously dabbing at the puddle. I could see he was in one of his moods again. Italians are famous for their volcanic tempers as well as their taste for coffee, and my father was no exception. One minute he would be laughing and dancing around the room like a demented sorcerer, the next he'd be troubled and unreachable.

"It'll be OK," I tried to reassure him. "I mean, with your work. Something will come up . . . eventually."

His face clouded, despite my best efforts. I could see that the strain of the last few years had taken its toll on him. As he peered out through the lace curtains onto the cobbled street, his olive skin, normally smooth and clear, looked gray and etched with worry.

Three years ago everything had been very different. Papa had been one of the most celebrated car designers of his age—along with his best friend and collaborator, the dashing Christian Silvestre.

Christian was an engineer, adventurer, part-time racing driver and, to me, all-around hero. Tall and handsome, with flashing teeth like a film star, he was rarely seen without a glass of champagne in his hand or sporting his trademark flying jacket.

Together, he and my father invented something the world had never seen before. Not only was their new car devilishly handsome, with its long, smooth curves and glinting chrome, it also had a unique secret hiding place under its bonnet. My father had sneaked me into his workshop to have a look, wearing just my pajamas and slippers. I craned to look underneath at the car's gleaming axles, and then my eyes had bulged like saucers as he breathlessly revealed the car's secret weapon.

Instead of being propelled by the wheels at the back like other cars, here was something altogether different: it was driven by the ones at the front. Christian insisted the new design would make the car much faster round corners, something he'd learned from his days competing in the Monte Carlo Rally.

The car had one other fiendish trick up its sleeve. Christian had devised a cunning button that would lock the back doors automatically so children couldn't open them while the car was moving.

When the car was finally unveiled at the 1934 Paris Motor Show, its daring new design kicked up a firestorm, almost as if my father and Christian had reinvented the wheel. The public went wild, immediately buying the car in droves.

Actually, that last bit wasn't entirely true. Back then, in the winter of 1934, only a tiny sliver of the population could afford the luxury of a car. Most people in France were dirt-poor and lived in the countryside. For them, buying a car was a bit like winning a ticket to Mars: it just wasn't going to happen. Instead, they had to make do with anything they could lay their hands on—horses, carts, bicycles . . . even knackered old donkeys. Especially knackered old donkeys.

But rich people in towns all over the country, from Toulouse to Tours, went crazy for my father's car.

It was official. His new design was a sensation!

All this was three long years ago, though. Since then, I'd watched Papa and Christian struggle time and again to repeat the success of their earlier invention. But somehow the magic kept eluding them. As each new motor show came along, other cars began to steal the limelight.

For several years now, under the new German Chancellor, Adolf Hitler, Germany had begun building a network of superfast roads they called autobahns—motorways. With no speed limit to speak of, the way was clear for a new breed of luxury limousine capable of reaching unheard-of speeds. Already, one of the country's biggest car companies, Mercedes, was developing just such a monster—a great Goliath of a car with a long, aggressive bonnet and streamlined wheel arches.

Against this kind of competition, my father seemed powerless. No amount of sugar in his coffee could make any difference. As each year turned into the next, he spent more and more time at his workshop, desperately trying to recreate the winning formula of that first astonishing car. But the more he tried, the more he failed . . . and the more he became lost to me.

It wasn't just me either. I can't remember the first time I noticed how much my parents were arguing, but after a while there was no mistaking it. They really didn't like each other anymore.

There were also the rumors I heard at the factory. For as long as I can remember my father had talked about people called the Money Men. I wasn't entirely sure what that meant—just that they had plenty of it and had poured it into the company.

At first, the Money Men were happy. But with money rapidly running out, these shadowy figures were now muttering in dark corners.

When there was no new success to speak of, the Money Men wanted a change . . . or their money back.

As far as I could see, only one thing could put everything right. One thing alone could save my father's career, rescue the company, and stop my parents splitting up.

We had to win the Paris Motor Show again.

My father looked up from the puddle of coffee that was now rapidly staining the tablecloth, and smiled sadly.

"Go and buy yourself a pastry from the bakery, Angelo," he sighed, pushing a few coins across the table.

I knew it was just his way of getting rid of me, but for once I didn't argue. Maybe my mother was right—it was better to leave him to wallow in his gloom.

Clutching the money in my hand, I hurried across the shiny cobbled streets to the pâtisserie. When I got there, I found a large queue of disgruntled customers already clogging the doorway. I wormed my way through to the front as the shop owner, a burly man with a handlebar mustache, tried to pacify the crowd.

"I'm sorry, but the ovens have not heated up yet. My good-for-nothing, and soon-to-be-fired, assistant forgot to turn them on." As he said the words, he glowered at the cowering assistant—a gangly youth in an oversized cap.

The assembled customers muttered disapprovingly as

they cast long looks at the glass counter. There was no denying it: the pastries were as flat as pancakes.

"They are beyond rescue," continued the shop owner rather dramatically. "You will all have to come back later."

The grumbling customers started to shuffle their way out the door.

All except me.

I had my eyes firmly fixed on a giant gougère. This was a favorite of mine, a savory pastry made from the same choux dough they used in éclairs but full of oozing cheese. Having suffered a similar fate to the other pastries, it was now lying discarded on a baking tray. But as I peered at it through the glass of the counter, I could just as easily have been staring at a holy relic.

"Please," I whispered urgently. "This one . . . I'll take it." The shopkeeper shot me a suspicious look, but I finally persuaded him that I was serious.

Hardly able to breathe, I handed over my coins before turning and fleeing. As I sprinted back across the street, the last of the autumn leaves whirled and danced around my feet—almost as if they knew that something magical was in the air.

By the time I had skidded through the door into the café, my father was pulling on his overcoat, ready to head back to his workshop.

"Wait, please!" I spluttered, barring his way. "You can't go!"

"What are you talking about?" Papa asked, irritated. "Angelo, I need to go to work. And you need to get to school."

"You don't understand," I protested. "I've found your new

car! Look!" I placed the cheese pastry on the table in front of him.

For a second my father stared at me like I was some kind of lunatic before finally turning to look at the gougère. Then, slowly, he picked it up and held it to the light, examining it from all angles.

"Do you see?" I asked impatiently.

Still my father didn't answer. Then, to the astonishment of the other customers, who were all gawping at us, open-mouthed, he took out his penknife and slowly, carefully, began to prod the pastry, pressing and smoothing its edges.

Thanks to the cool oven, the pastry had failed to rise fully, just as the shopkeeper had warned. But not all over: only at one end. As a result, it had taken on a lopsided shape. From one angle it was proudly domed in the traditional style, but from another, it sloped away where it had slumped, un-cooked. You could say it was almost aerodynamic.

For my father, like me, it was nothing short of a miracle. Until now, cars had almost always had long, angular bonnets with squared-off radiator grilles that looked like the front of stately homes. But this would be unlike anything anyone had ever seen before.

Here at last was the styling breakthrough my father had been groping for!

He turned slowly and looked me straight in the eye. "Angelo," he whispered. "You are a genius."

2 A Year Later

"Angelo!"

I lifted my welding visor and saw Madame Detrice, the boss's secretary, scowling indulgently at me from the doorway as she tapped at her fob watch. "You'll be late."

The boss, Bertrand Hipaux (pronounced like hippo, but without the "h"), was a retiring man who preferred others to take the limelight. Tall and willowy, with small, owlish glasses and a habit of wearing crumpled suits, he was probably in his early sixties. He'd never actually told me his age, but I'd worked it out from all the stories he'd told me about his days flying reconnaissance planes in the war.

Slightly shambling in his three-piece woolen suit and trademark trilby hat, he was a staunch believer in hard work and thrift. Not for him, Christian's world of fast cars and even faster women.

Bertrand had apparently decided that my father was a disaster when it came to organization. His mind, he said, worked not in a straight, or even a curved line, but in a squiggle like a rat's tail. Christian was no better. So the hyper-organized Madame Detrice had been dispatched to the workshop to run their lives for them. And now mine.

I flipped off the switch on my welding lamp, and the flame was immediately sucked back into the handle. Quick as a flash, I tugged off my apron and set off to find Papa.

Ever since the day when I had inspired him with a lop-sided pastry, he'd allowed me into his workshop before school, to see the new car take shape.

The workshop was my favorite place in the whole world. Stepping inside was like finding you'd strayed into the laboratory of some fiendish wizard. Every surface was festooned with crazy drawings, formulas, designs, doodles and posters—diagrams of every description, yet always of one thing: vehicles. Not always cars either—trains, motorbikes, airplanes, rocket-propelled missiles . . . anything and everything, so long as it went fast.

In the center of the room was a series of wooden worktops—not that you could see them. They were covered, sometimes nearly a foot deep, in all the junk of engineering and drawing. Slabs of modeling clay were kept moist with sheets of damp newspaper, some dating back decades; in fact, back as far as the Great War—the last time the German army had invaded France.

There were also welding lamps, helmets, goggles, pencils,

strange measuring calipers, knives, abandoned coffee cups and discarded wine bottles—all the equipment required for fantastical invention.

Oh, and not forgetting sugar, of course. Secret hoards of the stuff were squirreled away in drawers already bulging with half-eaten pastries and long-forgotten fondants.

As soon as I arrived each morning, my father would equip me with a pair of greasy overalls to put over my uniform, a leather apron around my waist and a pair of goggles. I would now be ready to get to work on the piles of old scrap metal he kept to one side for me. Old cans, lighter cases, springs, coils, cogs and broken paneling—you name it, it was all here.

Next came the moment I loved more than all else: firing up the welding torch itself. As the flame hissed into life, it flashed white off the glass of my goggles and I set about working and reworking the metal scraps into fantastical creations—usually some sort of prototype for my own car of the future.

Most mornings, when Madame Detrice tried to shoo me off to school, I would try to find some way to eke out a few extra minutes—anything to put off going to that medieval torture chamber, as I called it. But even when I sprinted all the way to school, somehow I would always arrive late. Which meant only one thing: a whipping from old Crespin, the headmaster.

Today, however, was different. Today there would be no school, because in just over one hour the 1938 Paris Motor Show would finally be opening its doors and I would be there to see it.

Like a World Cup for car designers, the motor show was the most important event in the motoring calendar. The world's leading industrial tycoons, designers, film stars and journalists would all be converging to marvel at the latest and greatest cars on display. And my father's new design would have pride of place.

Since the fateful day nearly a year ago when I had stumbled across the sunken pastry, Papa had worked tirelessly, often late into the night, sculpting and resculpting his new creation. Like the pastry, the car had a totally unique shape, one that I was convinced the newspapers would take to their hearts. Domed at the front, it had a massive bonnet with lizard-like eyes sticking out at the sides, and a roof that curved away to a thin wafer at the back.

But, of course, its real party trick lay underneath. As well as front-wheel drive, Christian had given the car hydro-pneumatic suspension. I'd watched him testing it in the workshop. At rest, the car sagged down at the back, the rear fenders almost scraping the ground. But when the key was put into the ignition and turned two notches, the car rose on a cushion of air, just like the pastry that had inspired it.

The new feature meant that the car was much smoother driving over the cobbled streets of Paris, a luxury that was bound to go down well with the elegant ladies my mother lunched with.

This was the car my father and I were pinning all our hopes on, the design that would make him famous again and solve all our problems.

My heart racing with anticipation, I tugged open the sliding wooden doors of the workshop and ran across the yard toward the factory, skipping across rail tracks that glinted in the early-morning sun.

Ahead lay the doors to the main factory floor, where workers had once produced over two hundred cars a day. Not that they were making anything like that quantity anymore.

Strictly speaking, I wasn't allowed to go inside. Bristling with huge metal smelting machinery and cars dangling from overhead conveyor belts, it was a perilous place for its army of cloth-capped, sooty-faced workers, let alone for a wide-eyed boy of thirteen.

Today, however, I threw caution to the wind. As I stole through the door, I was hit by a wall of heat that scalded my cheeks. The noise and smells were overwhelming too—a deafening clanking of metal hammers and drilling mixed with the stench of sweat and molten metal. To think that before long this army would be hard at work building my father's latest design!

My eyes scanned the factory floor until I spotted Papa huddled in a corner with Christian. For a moment I was struck by just how comical they looked together: Christian so tall and athletic-looking, my father stocky and dark with his broad, flat forehead, like some foraging creature you half expected to crash out of a bush at any moment.

As I made my way over, I realized that Papa was annoyed, arguing with Christian over something to do with the exhibition.

"What do you mean we're in the corner?" he growled. "How will anyone see us if we're stuck in a broom cupboard?"

Before he could answer, Christian spotted me and nodded

to my father, who spun round and glared at me irritably. "What are you doing in here? You know you should be at school."

"At school?" I spluttered. "But surely I'm coming with you to the show—"

"It's out of the question," my father snapped. "Your mother will kill me. You know how she gets if you miss any classes."

"Surely Angelo can afford to skip school just this once?" Christian tried to protest.

But Papa was too preoccupied to hear any arguments. "It's impossible. Now hurry, before you're late." With that, he turned his back on me so that he could carry on poring over the designs for the little display plinth the car was going to sit on.

For a moment I stood completely still, too winded to move. I burned inside with the sheer injustice of it. Hadn't it been my discovery of the pastry that had helped inspire the new design? What's more, I knew that my father despised my school almost as much as I did. It was something he and Maman always rowed about.

So why was he insisting I go now? Today of all days? I suspected the real reason was nothing to do with my mother or the school. He just didn't want me to see him humiliated if something went wrong at the show.

Even if I'd wanted to argue, I knew there was no point. Once Papa had set his mind on something, that was it. He was as stubborn as a mule.

"Good luck." I sighed forlornly. "They're going to love it." Then I skulked off toward school, not even caring if I was whipped for being late.

I left the factory and kicked a stone dejectedly along the embankment, not even looking up when I reached the rows of bookstalls that lined the Seine. Usually I was drawn magnetically to these stalls, with their treasure troves of postcards, etchings and paintings. But not today. I turned right and made my way gloomily along the backstreets hidden behind the grand courtyards that housed many of the city's universities.

Next I cut right again, across a large open market that bordered a warren of poorer, dirtier streets beyond. Here all life was teeming—greengrocers were crying out the prices of fruit as bicycle delivery carts jostled with omnibuses and horse-drawn wagons stacked impossibly high with crates of vegetables, hay and rope. One of the city's earliest road-sweeping trucks shuddered past, spraying my boots with filthy water as it churned up the rotting cabbage leaves and straw. Staggering back, I was very nearly trampled under the hooves of a police horse, which earned me a stern rebuke from the officer trying to control the traffic chaos.

Suddenly I heard a cry high above the other voices. At first I thought it was one of the fruit sellers, but after a few more shouts I realized that someone was calling my name.

"Angelo!"

I spun round, peering through the jostling crowds to see who could be calling me. Then, all at once, I saw the glint of metal handlebars, and a vintage BMW motorbike and sidecar burst through the crowd and pulled up beside me. Sitting astride it was my father.

"Get in," he cried. "If we hurry, we can still make it in time."

"Make what?" I asked, bewildered. Surely he wasn't planning on driving me to school.

"The motor show, of course."

"But I thought—"

"I was stupid," he interrupted. "Of course you must be there. Here!"

He threw me the spare helmet, and next thing I knew I was clambering into the sidecar as fast as I could. With a sharp twist of the throttle, the motorbike produced a loud crack like a shotgun, then roared across the square, belching a plume of black smoke in its wake. Grinning from ear to ear, I glanced back in time to see the irate police officer clutch a handkerchief to his face to stop himself from choking.

Moments later we were sailing over the nearby bridge, tires squealing as we banked left.

Ahead of us loomed the Grand Palais, where the motor show was already opening its doors.

3 The 1938 Paris Motor Show

I stopped in my tracks and stared, openmouthed. Spread out before me was a truly wondrous sight. High above, the glass of the enormous vaulted ceiling sparkled dazzlingly in the sunlight. Below, as far as the eye could see, the exhibition hall was bursting with every type of car, from the most experimental three-wheeled contraption to vehicles that looked more like luxury ocean liners. All our major rivals were here, showing off their latest projects, some so futuristic they looked like they'd been torn out of the pages of a science fiction comic.

My father gasped. "Come on," he said. "We need to hurry."

As we made our way across, I gaped at the lavish displays the other car companies had mounted. At one, a group of dancing girls dressed as cinema usherettes handed out free bonbons and souvenirs.

In the middle of the hall, center stage, stood the display for one of my father's biggest German rivals. A small, wiry man in a tight woolen suit, clutching a leather briefcase, was busy fussing around the stand. I recognized him from a newspaper article Papa had once shown me. I didn't know his name, but I knew he was the enemy—or at least my father's rival, his direct counterpart in Germany.

Suddenly there was a commotion as a group of senior executives ushered someone important into the hall. I craned forward on tiptoe, but all I glimpsed was a long black raincoat and a broad felt hat.

"Porsche," my father muttered darkly in my ear. I had often heard him mention the name. Dr. Ferdinand Porsche was one of the most highly revered engineers in the world.

"Who's that with him?" I asked. Several powerful-looking men in somber suits and trilby hats cleared the crowds in Porsche's path.

"Nazis," Papa told me, spitting the word out with contempt. I felt a shiver run down my neck. For years now, all the newspapers had been talking about was how the Nazis were building up a huge army ready to invade the rest of Europe.

Somehow no one wanted to believe that another war was possible. For people like my father's boss, Bertrand, the memory of the last time the German army had swept over France's border was all too fresh.

"Come on." My father grabbed my arm and led me across to the other side of the hall.

Once we'd weaved our way through the glitz of the other displays, past the usherettes handing out free sweets, and even a performing bear, we finally arrived at ours.

It's true that compared to some of the other stands, it was a humble affair. Yet my breath was completely taken away. There in front of me was the car I had helped to create all those months ago. The car that had started out as a lopsided pastry.

I stepped toward it, spellbound. It was unique, all right—in fact, it was without doubt the finest, shiniest, most perfect piece of craftsmanship I had ever seen. I let my fingers trail over the soft lines of its bodywork, its gleaming chrome fenders and headlamps, to its bulging windscreen and the black canvas hood that sloped away to a thin wedge at the back. If I hadn't been close to tears of astonishment, I would have laughed out loud at just how similar to a sunken pie it looked.

"It's beautiful," I whispered.

"You may think that," my father remarked with a sniff, "but will any of this lot?" He peered across the hall at the crowds of visitors and journalists now swarming around the other displays. "Will they even notice it?" He sighed gloomily.

Suddenly a figure pushed through the crowd and grabbed my father's arm.

"Where have you been?" Christian asked hoarsely.

"I had to make a small detour," Papa explained, "but I'm here now. Not that there was much point."

"Don't worry," Christian assured him with a mysterious glint in his eye. "I've arranged something to help show the car off in . . . how shall I put it? A better light." With that, a young woman draped in a large gray overcoat came forward. "This is Béatrice," he announced proudly.

The young woman smiled and held out a hand. "Pleased to meet you," she purred coyly.

But it was as though my father hadn't even seen her. "The display is a disaster," he grumbled.

"Stop worrying," Christian urged him. "I have a secret weapon." He turned and nodded toward the girl. "Béatrice is a dancer."

On cue, she opened her overcoat, and my mouth fell slack like a goldfish's. She was wearing nothing but a sequined swimming costume covered in shiny tassels.

My father stared at her blankly, then turned to Christian, who was grinning like a puppy. "I'm getting some coffee," he grunted before stalking off in fury.

For the briefest of seconds, Christian's smile faltered; then he turned back to Béatrice, oozing confidence again. "He loves it," he assured her. "Why don't you get started?"

Béatrice began to strip off her overcoat and pin on a large, tawdry headdress. Unsure where to look, I let my eyes stray across the hall to where Papa was now having a heated conversation with Bertrand.

I worshipped "Uncle" Bertrand. When my father first arrived in Paris hoping to make his fortune, Bertrand had seen his drawings and given him a job on the spot. I remember asking years later what had made him take on a penniless artist with so little formal training. Bertrand looked at me with soft, twinkling eyes and shrugged. "I saw something in your father more important than qualifications." He smiled. "I saw passion. And with passion, anything is possible."

Over the years Bertrand grew to be much more than just my father's boss—he became my unofficial godfather, a stand-in for the grandfathers back in Italy whom I never saw.

But as I watched his eyes scouring the hall, taking in the grandeur of all the other displays, I could see that Bertrand was worried. Over at the German stand, the crowds were pressing and shoving like bees round honey. At ours there still wasn't a soul.

I sighed heavily and wandered over.

As soon as he saw me, Bertrand's eyes lit up and he pulled me into a huge bear hug. "My dear boy." He beamed, hiding any trace of his worried expression. "So you've bunked off school, have you? Only right that our top designer should be here."

"Except everyone's over at the German stand," I complained.

"Can you blame them?" came a rich, gravelly voice from behind me.

I spun round to find Ferdinand Porsche himself approaching, flanked by his Nazi heavies. A gaunt hand shot out from under his cape.

"Bertrand," he croaked with a cold smile. "I'd almost forgotten you were going to be here."

I could see Bertrand's jaw tighten with dislike as he made no effort to shake the hand. Just behind him, my father was hurrying back with his coffee, clearly disturbed to see us talking to the enemy.

"As I was explaining to my young friend here," Bertrand answered Porsche coolly, "I prefer to let craftsmanship speak for itself."

"Then it had better speak a little more loudly," the German engineer said with a smirk. "Because at the moment I'm not hearing anything."

I could see Papa's face darken with anger as he overheard the slight, but before he could say anything, the wiry little man with the briefcase and spectacles appeared at Porsche's side.

"Herr Porsche," he whispered, shuffling nervously. "We're ready for you to make your speech."

Porsche grunted, then threw a look toward my father. "It's Fabrizzi, isn't it?"

"What if it is?" Papa snarled.

"Your last car was most unusual. If you ever need a job, be sure to give my assistant a call."

With that he swept off to deliver his speech. His assistant gave us an awkward half smile, nodding like a bird pecking at the ground for a worm, then scurried after his boss.

"Arrogant monkey!" my father hissed furiously.

"You should be flattered," Bertrand told him. "Someone as powerful as him admiring your work!"

"I'd sooner have this lot admiring it." Papa scowled, glaring at the crowds that were surging toward the German stand to listen to Porsche's speech.

"They will," Bertrand soothed.

"When?" my father snapped impatiently.

"Some things aren't meant to be," Bertrand assured him. "The rest aren't meant to be yet."

A few moments later I found myself back at our stand. Despite Béatrice's preparations for her dance routine, the entire hall was now listening, rapt, to Porsche's speech.

I sighed heavily. If only there was something I could do to attract more attention to our car. If people could just see what it was capable of—especially its futuristic suspension—surely the crowds would flock round.

There was nothing for it. I would have to take matters into my own hands. As stealthily as I could, I clambered up onto the stand and reached for the car's glinting door handle. To my surprise, it clicked open without protest. My pulse quickening, I glanced around furtively. Across the hall my father was still deep in discussion with Bertrand, while Christian was trying to persuade a photographer to come over and take Béatrice's picture.

It was now or never. I eased the door open and sank into the soft leather of the driving seat. In front of me, the controls spread out invitingly like the flight deck of a space rocket. Sticking out at right angles to the steering wheel, almost like a joystick, was the transmission lever itself. With the engine running, one pull and the car would almost literally become airborne.

Unaware of my presence, Béatrice was now ready to begin her routine. Adopting a kittenish pose, she draped her body across the bonnet and drew her lips into a little pout.

The effect was instantaneous. One by one, several grizzled journalists began to nudge each other and peel away from the German stand. Soon a small crowd had gathered, gawping, transfixed. As Béatrice continued to wriggle around on the bonnet, I spotted the photographer Christian had been talking to wrestle his way to the front and raise his camera. There was a loud crunch of phosphorous and the bulb exploded, blinding me with a searing flash.

It took several moments for my eyesight to recover, but when it did I had to blink three times to reassure myself I wasn't seeing things. There in front of me, already sitting in the ignition, was the car key. . . .

I swallowed hard. It was exactly the chance I'd been looking for. Now at last I could show the car off in all its glory.

Cautiously, I turned the key a quarter notch. No sooner had I done so than there was a squeal of rubber on glass and the wipers jerked to life. My shaking hands must have nudged the tiny windscreen wiper switch. While my heartbeat recovered from the shock, my eyes followed the wipers as they arced across the windscreen in a rhythmic pulse. It was hardly the spectacular display I'd been hoping for.

I now knew what I had to do. Steadying my nerves, I switched off the wipers, reached forward and turned the key one further click.

As if by magic, the back of the car rose on a cushion of air as the suspension stirred from its sleep. I felt myself float nearly a foot into the air, and my heart swelled with pride at this marvel of engineering.

Béatrice's pout immediately faltered and she threw a confused glance over her shoulder at me. But I wasn't bothered: the crowd gathered around were delighted by this new turn of events and burst into spontaneous applause. Even Ferdinand Porsche was looking over, annoyed by the competition.

Inside the cockpit, I was just about to congratulate myself

on a job well done, when a warning light started to flash on the dashboard. Soon it was joined by another, this time beeping insistently.

If I was feeling pleased with myself before, I could now feel a prickle of fear tug at my collar. Something was definitely wrong. Urging myself to remain calm, I began pressing buttons faster and faster in the vague hope that one of them would cure the problem. They didn't.

Suddenly I heard a loud click and froze. One of the buttons had triggered the child lock system, and now even the driver's door refused to budge. Trouble was, I'd pressed so many buttons I didn't know which one to unpress. I began urgently pulling at the door handle to override the locking system, but it was no use.

By now Christian had clambered up onto the plinth and was peering in through the windscreen. "Angelo? Is that you?" I saw him mouth.

I nodded furiously, but through the thick glass I could barely hear a word.

He tried saying something again, but he was drowned out by a brass band that had suddenly struck up the German national anthem over at the German stand.

Bewildered, I convinced myself that Christian was telling me to turn the key again. Of course! The warning light must be the battery. If it was running low, I would need to start the engine to restore the power. I reached for the key, and as I gave it one last turn, the car's engine growled to life.

Suddenly I saw Christian's eyes widen in alarm. He shook his head furiously, but it only made me more confused than ever. Sensing real danger now, I began frantically tugging at the door again, but as I did so, my elbow must have nudged the transmission lever and it shunted down into drive.

With a rasp of metal cogs, the gears engaged and the car surged forward. Terrified, I stamped on the brake as hard as I could, but it was too late. . . .

For a moment Béatrice was surfing through empty space as the car launched itself off the plinth, scattering the press in all directions. A second later it plunged down onto the parquet floor, twisting off its fenders and splitting the radiator grille, before finally crunching into the next-door stand.

As the dust finally settled, the crowd peered over the up-turned tables and stared, agog. Porsche himself was watching, utterly bemused. Even the brass band had stopped playing the German anthem and were gaping, openmouthed.

Inside the car, I slumped back and blinked in astonishment. Feeling something warm trickling down my forehead, I dabbed at it and found I was bleeding from a little cut from where my head had glanced off the steering wheel. Other than that I was OK.

So too, amazingly, was the car—apart from the small geyser of steam hissing from the radiator. Oh, and the puddle of oil oozing from a crack in the suspension.

What I didn't know, however, was that directly above me there was a much bigger car, balanced on a taller plinth. And now it was starting to teeter. . . .

My father, who had barged his way through the crowds to the front, saw the danger first and made a superhuman lunge to get me free. But it was too late. . . . With a sickening shudder, the car above me lurched forward and toppled off its stand.

Directly underneath, my eyes bulged wildly as I saw the huge shape bearing down on me. Before Papa or Christian could do anything, the car nosedived straight onto the roof above me, crushing it like tinfoil.

What no one outside could have known, however, was that in the split second before impact I had had the sense to dive behind the rear seats. As I tried to squirm my way into the boot, one of my legs trailed behind me and missed being crushed flat by a hairsbreadth.

For a moment I sat, rigid with fear, in the boot compartment, straining to hear. Why was it so silent? Could it be I was dead already?

Suddenly I heard the sound of hammering and tugging at every door before the boot was prized open and a pair of arms hauled me out. Seconds later I was being crushed half senseless in the arms of my father, who was chanting prayers in some unintelligible dialect from his home village in Italy.

As he hugged me to him, squeezing out what little air was left inside me, I managed to catch a glimpse of the car over his shoulder.

Where once it had been lopsided, it was now as flat as a pancake.

4 What Happened Next

Bertrand stood gloomily by the window of his office, a large paneled room full of somber furniture in the west wing of the factory. My father and I had come to see him in the aftermath of the previous morning's events. Since my disaster with the car, I'd tried to apologize to Papa, but it was hopeless. He couldn't bring himself to look at me, let alone talk.

On top of all this, the night before, my parents had had the worst row I'd ever heard. Their arguments often ended up with a plate crashing against the wall or a slammed door. But this was different. Maman had been shouting that I should never have gone to the motor show in the first place. Apparently, Crespin, my headmaster, had rung up to say I was suspended for skipping school. For my mother, this seemed to be far more of a disaster than what I'd done to the car.

My father had shouted back that he didn't give two figs about the school—he'd never wanted me to go there in the first place. That made Maman retaliate that he should thank goodness that her father still paid the fees. She often liked to throw this at my father to humiliate him.

Shortly after, I heard the front door slam and then my mother crying softly. When I looked out the window, I saw Papa hurry onto the street, pulling on his jacket furiously. It wasn't until the early hours of the morning that I heard him slip quietly back in.

Maybe, just maybe, everything would still be all right. If I apologized enough to Bertrand, explained that it had all been my fault, disaster could be averted.

As I stood waiting in his office, I felt my neck prickle with tension where the coarse material of the collar rubbed. Whenever I was in trouble, I would always start tugging at my collar.

After a moment Bertrand turned, his hooded eyes heavy with sadness. "The board have called an emergency meeting." He sighed.

"What kind of emergency?" I asked sheepishly.

"They're thinking about sacking me," my father explained grimly.

"Absolutely not!" Bertrand insisted. "But it may be a good idea if you take a little leave." He rummaged in a drawer for his pipe and wedged it in his mouth without lighting it. "My house in the country is sitting empty. Take it for a few weeks' holiday while I sort things out here."

My father smiled ruefully and shook his head again. "I don't think a holiday is what I need."

"I'm serious," Bertrand urged him. "You need the rest. Besides, Angelo would enjoy it."

I wanted to say that I didn't feel I deserved anything except a sound flogging from Crespin. But I thought better of it and kept silent.

"I wouldn't know what to do with myself," my father said eventually, with a shrug. "I'd die of boredom."

Bertrand didn't pursue it any further, and my heart sank. I dreaded to think what would happen to us now. I'd seen how Papa's mood could become black when things were bad. But this was worse than anything before. I had to say something.

"Please," I blurted. "This is all my fault."

Bertrand shook his head solemnly. "No, Angelo. Our problems started long before yesterday morning."

He rested his hand on my father's shoulder. "Take the house. For me."

"Maybe we should, Papa," I ventured hopefully. I kept thinking that my mother would enjoy it. A holiday might make them get on again.

"Life is a pendulum swing," Bertrand tried to reassure him. "The good thing about being at the bottom is that you know it can only go up."

My father turned and stared mournfully at him. "Unless the clock has already stopped," he muttered. Then he turned and walked quietly out of the room.

A few hours later my father and I sat silently in the Petit Chemin de Fer, the faded little café behind the workshop, as my mother sipped her tea. I watched her lips purse round the edge of the china cup—lips that I remembered once as soft and warm, now brittle and drawn. There was a trace of old lipstick round the edge of the cup and she grimaced and put it down.

"What will you do now?" she asked my father eventually.

He glanced out onto the street, looking haunted. "Bertrand has offered to let us stay in his house near Bordeaux for a few weeks to ride out the storm."

"What about Angelo's school?" Maman asked sharply.

"I'm not going back there," I interrupted. "Why can't I go to the local school like normal people?" The local school filled my mother with horror because we lived in one of the poorer districts of Paris. It had taken her nearly a year of petitioning to get me into a school in another, better-off area.

She turned to my father, her eyes steely with anger. "I will not have him going to a local school. I've spoken to Monsieur Crespin, and he's agreed that Angelo can come back so long as he apologizes."

"Never," I hissed, earning a sharp scowl from my mother.

"You'll do as you're told," she snapped.

I fell silent, my eyes drifting miserably to my undrunk chocolate.

"Maybe Bertrand's right," Maman sighed. "A spell apart might be good for all of us."

Papa shot her a furious look. "Now isn't the time to discuss this."

"He needs to know," she hissed.

"Know what?" I asked. I could feel my guts clenching with panic. I looked from one parent to the other, half confused, half dreading what I already suspected. "Wait . . .

You're splitting up?" I whispered, barely daring to say the words. "But you can't . . ."

"Not splitting up," my father tried to reassure me. "Just taking a break . . . to rethink our options."

I could see that my parents were avoiding looking each other in the eye.

"This is because of the car—?" I blurted.

"No," Papa tried to reassure me, but it was too late. I could feel my eyes brimming with hot tears. Humiliated by my childishness and blinded with anger at myself and my parents, I leaped to my feet, sending cutlery flying.

"Angelo!" my mother scolded me. "People are watching!"

"I don't care!" I raged, inadvertently sweeping my cup of chocolate to the floor. It smashed to pieces, spraying dark ooze like mud up the window. My mother gasped, and even I was taken aback by my outburst.

But it was too late to back out now. I threw down my napkin and ran out of the café, leaving the rest of the customers speechless.

It was a full three hours later, long after my dinner had gone cold, that my father eased open the workshop door and found me hunched in the corner against one of the benches. He slumped down next to me, and for a while we sat in silence.

Eventually I heard him clear his throat. "Angelo—"

I interrupted before he could go any further. "Don't try and say this isn't my fault, because it is. If I hadn't turned that key, none of this would have happened."

"Life is always full of ifs," he sighed. "I know you wanted

things to be different . . . but not everything is within our control."

"That car was."

"Maybe," he admitted. "But not what happened with your mother and me. I'm afraid that crashed and burned all by itself."

I looked up at him, a sense of hopelessness engulfing me. "Is there really no chance . . . ?"

He put his arm round me and smiled. "Let's get through the next two weeks and see then."

I knew there was no use pushing the matter further—except maybe on one point.

"If you go, I'm coming with you," I insisted.

My father studied me in the tiny sliver of moonlight that had found its way through a crack in the window. "Do I have a choice?"

I shook my head and he sighed ruefully. "Your mother will kill me . . . again."

"Tell her I'll go back to school as soon as we return."

He glanced at me, raising a skeptical eyebrow. "You promise?"

"I said tell her I will. I didn't say I'd actually do it."

We stared at each other for a moment before sharing a conspiratorial smile. . . .

It was true. I had no intention of returning to my school—after the fortnight at Bertrand's house, or ever.

5 The House in the Country

It was midnight when my father's ancient motorbike rattled to a halt outside the gates of Bertrand's holiday home, buried deep in the countryside of southwest France. Huddled in the sidecar, swathed in blankets to keep out the cold, my bones shaken almost into powder, I peered at the manor house looming out of the darkness. It was more like a château really, grim and forbidding in the moonlight, a crumbling old pile with rickety shutters, sitting in several acres of vineyards at the top of a gently sloping hill.

"It looks deserted," I grumbled, trying to be heard over the exhaust backfiring. Just then I saw a light come on, and an elderly woman came to the door and gestured for us to go round to the side entrance. A second later my head was snapped back as my father released the clutch and we lurched off through the gate and across the gravel court-yard.

A bolt on the side door slid back with a rusty squeal to reveal the woman. She was broad-hipped and muscular, and closer inspection revealed that she was younger than I'd thought—maybe only in her forties. Her face had tough-ened like leather from what must have been years of hard toil, and her mouth was set in a stern grimace. A single curl of coarse black hair grew out of a mole on her chin.

Papa flashed her his brightest smile. "We had a few prob-lems with the engine," he explained.

"Sometimes it forgets to work," I chimed in for good mea-sure. But if I was hoping for a flicker of warmth in return, I was to be disappointed.

The woman glanced dubiously at the motorbike, then at my grimy face staring out from the blankets and goggles. Then she jerked her head to the side to indicate that we should follow her.

"You're Marguerite, Bertrand's housekeeper?" my father asked politely.

She nodded, motioning for us to follow her along the corridor. I hung back for a moment with my father.

"Why won't she speak to us?" I hissed suspiciously.

"I don't think she can—Bertrand said that she's been mute for years," he replied, before setting off after her.

At the end of the hall, we took the wide stone staircase to the first floor, where Marguerite unlocked a door to reveal a sparsely furnished bedroom with floor-to-ceiling shutters and a fireplace that looked like it hadn't been used for de-cades. She lit a candle, then left, still without saying a word.

A moment or two later, my father pulled the shutters back an inch and we watched her crunch her way across the forecourt and out of the main gates.

"We have the place to ourselves," Papa sighed.

Five minutes later we were curled up together in the center of the bed, both still in our outdoor coats and swaddled in scarves. My teeth chattering, I could feel the cold slowly creeping into my bones from the rock-hard mattress underneath.

Maybe coming on "holiday" hadn't been such a good idea after all.

The following morning I woke early, feeling damp and stiff. My father was still snoring loudly beside me, so I decided to slip out and explore the grounds.

Downstairs, I had to lean all my weight against the front door to get it to shift more than a few inches. When I finally managed to squeeze through the gap, I discovered that it had snowed in the night, settling in a drift against the door. Stepping gingerly across the thin layer of white, I peered around the courtyard and spotted some derelict outbuildings, overgrown with weeds; huddled in the corner was an old garage.

After I prized the door open, it seemed to take forever for my eyes to adjust to the darkness. But when they did, a smile slowly spread across my face. Lurking in the shadows in the corner was an ancient blue tractor. That wasn't all. Behind it, buried under a mountain of tennis rackets and croquet mallets, was an old ride-on lawn mower.

I was about to jump into the seat when the sound of a gate creaking on its hinges made me turn. I darted my head back outside and saw the housekeeper hurrying in through the snow, her gray shawl wrapped around her head as she leaned into the frosty wind. I dragged the garage door shut behind me and made my way back across the icy courtyard.

"Am I glad to see you!" I called to the woman as I burst in through the door. "I'm starving."

The figure turned, and to my shock I realized it wasn't Marguerite at all but a girl, possibly only a year older than myself. Her skin was so clear it was almost luminous, while her ruby lips were chapped and split from the bitter cold.

"Who are you?" she demanded, her piercing green eyes staring at me, full of fierce suspicion.

"Er . . . Angelo," I stammered. "My father and I are staying here for a few weeks."

The girl looked me up and down, clearly unimpressed, then unwound the scarf. A mane of thick, unruly red hair spilled onto her shoulders.

"What happened to Marguerite?" I asked, suddenly a little tongue-tied.

"I help her out when there are visitors." She took off her coat and tied an apron tightly round her waist. "Don't expect much to eat, by the way. The delivery van broke an axle in Boutonne when it slid off the road, so there's only some stale bread."

"We could always take the motorbike to collect some fresh," I offered brightly. "How far is it to the nearest village?"

"Regnac is just the other side of the stream, but it doesn't have a bakery. You can sometimes get pastries at the bar tabac if you go early enough. Otherwise the nearest town is Boutonne," she explained. "But it's twenty kilometers away."

With that, she set about scouring the cupboards to prepare what little breakfast she could. I watched her for a moment before she felt my gaze on the back of her neck and turned fiercely.

"What?"

I shrank back like a scalded cat. "Nothing."

A little while later, after chewing on a rather meager breakfast of dried fruit and stale bread, I went outside to find my father trying to kick-start the motorbike. After a moment he cursed and aimed a sharp boot at the exhaust pipe.

"It's frozen solid. I knew I should have brought it inside." He looked over and saw me concealing a smile. "You think this is funny?"

"Come and see," I said, dragging him over to the rickety old shed.

I pulled open the huge wooden doors, and Papa's face lit up as he spotted the old tractor lurking in the back. Heading over, he wiped some dust off the radiator, and a chrome nameplate gleamed back at him.

"It's a Lamborghini!" he exclaimed. "We had one almost exactly the same when I was your age."

Intrigued, I ran my hands over the rusty bonnet, then suddenly froze. The key had been left in the ignition. "Maybe you should try it," I suggested cautiously.

My father leaped into the driver's seat and gave the key a turn.

Nothing. He tried again: still the same.

Marguerite's helper was right—we were indeed marooned. But as I turned to head out of the shed, I caught a glimpse of the lawn mower. . . .

Seconds later we burst out of the garage, my father holding on to the lawn mower's handlebars, goggles down, while I clung on behind, acting as rear gunner. Hearing the commotion, the girl came to the doorway and stared in bewilderment.

"We'll be back with some fresh pastries!" I shouted to her, rather too pleased with myself.

The lawn mower, however, had other ideas. At that precise moment it took an unexpected detour—straight toward the house. Seeing the danger, my father made a lunge for the brakes, only to find that the cables had snapped, presumably gnawed through by some rodent.

With seconds to spare, he wrenched the handlebars to the right, avoiding the stone wall by a whisker. Clattering dementedly toward the gate, we bounced through a puddle, squirting frozen mud up our fronts and completely covering my father's goggles.

"I can't see anything!" he shouted.

I leaned forward and wiped the lenses as best I could while he piloted the machine out through the gates and down the snow-covered track.

As we rattled our way down the hill, I peered around at the countryside flashing past. On either side the meadows were covered in snow, lilac in the early-morning light. A few cows, huddled together by a trough of frozen water, lifted their heads to see what the noise was about, then turned away, bored.

Suddenly we rounded a corner and I saw that we were rapidly approaching a stream. With no way round it and no time to stop, our only option was to carry straight on through.

"Go! Go!" I roared in Papa's ear.

He twisted the throttle and the lawn mower plunged into the stream, sending up a huge curtain of icy water in our wake. As we burst out the other side, we let out a huge whoop of excitement that sent a flock of starlings flapping up into the sky.

Ahead lay a daunting climb up to the village through an avenue of cypress trees. Urging the lawn mower on, my father squeezed every last bit of power out of the whining engine until, spluttering and coughing, we swept into the square.

To our left was the imposing structure of the church, its huge medieval tower casting a shadow over the entire hillside. On the other side, a pair of scruffy, peeling doors opened out onto the street from a dingy little café—the local bar tabac.

As we circled the muddy square, a thought suddenly popped into my head.

"If the brakes don't work, how do we stop?" I shouted over the racket the engine was making.

By now one or two of the locals had emerged from the bar and were watching our antics curiously. The same thought had obviously occurred to them. As we banked sharply for another fly-past, I nodded and lifted my cap in greeting.

"You'll have to switch it off!" I yelled in my father's ear. But he clearly couldn't hear over the noise of the engine. Worryingly, a low wall was now looming fast in front of us.

"Turn it off!" I shouted more urgently this time. Papa began searching desperately for any sign of an "off" button, but there wasn't one. With seconds to impact, I reached forward and snatched the key out of the ignition.

The sound—or lack of it—was instantly deafening as we

coasted forward, then shunted to an abrupt halt against the wall. With the morning's performance clearly at an end, the locals now melted back into the café as silently as they had emerged.

My father dusted himself off and peered at the bar in front of us. "Time for coffee," he announced cheerfully.

Inside, a rather portly man stood chatting to a small gathering of locals. This, it turned out, was Victor, the owner—a proud, stout figure who had cultivated a huge handlebar moustache that sprouted from under his bulbous nose like a pair of restless ferrets.

A woman appeared from a doorway behind him and started wiping down the tables. This, I would soon discover, was Dominique, his wife. Pale and delicate like an exotic flower, she glanced over at us, and I saw a flicker of curiosity before she averted her eyes shyly.

"Excuse me," my father called out to attract the barman's attention. The chatter of the other men hushed, and Victor looked over indifferently. "A black coffee, a hot chocolate and two tartines, if you will."

"Sorry," Victor grunted, without sounding the least bit sorry. "We're fresh out of bread."

"Perhaps if we come back later," my father suggested. "Are you expecting any deliveries?"

"Not for several days at least." The barman sniffed. "The delivery van is out of action." He set about preparing our drinks while the older men muttered conspiratorially, shooting glances our way.

"But why doesn't someone just drive to the nearest town?" I asked, confused.

At that the men at the end of the bar fell silent. As Victor shoved my hot chocolate across the counter, I sensed I had somehow touched a nerve.

"Perhaps you could drive your lawn mower," he suggested with a sly smile. Instantly I felt my cheeks burn with embarrassment.

"Can you at least tell us if there's a restaurant where we can eat?" my father asked, clearly frustrated now.

"Absolutely," Victor replied, more brightly this time. "You're sitting in it. But, before you ask, there's no menu."

I could sense the hairs rising on the back of my father's neck. "Then perhaps we can book a table for later."

"Of course. But you may have a long wait." Victor smirked. "We're shut until the spring." This brought a hearty roar from the rest of his cronies.

Papa's jaw tightened and he gulped his coffee down in one slurp. "Let's go," he hissed.

I tried to protest that I hadn't even started my chocolate yet, but he was already stalking out the door. As I turned to follow him, I saw the barman's wife watching me closely. For a moment I wondered if she was embarrassed by her husband's snide remarks. But if she was, she didn't say anything.

Outside, we wheeled the lawn mower round to face in the right direction; then I leaped on. Hastily grabbing my father's waist so I didn't topple off the back, I tugged my hat down over my mop of dark hair and we backfired our way across the square and headed toward the manor house.

Less than an hour later, I was squatting at the bottom of the big stone staircase. My father was on the telephone to my mother.

At first there were some hushed mutterings I could barely make out: something, I thought, about Ferdinand Porsche. I'd heard my father and Bertrand whispering a few days before about how Porsche was secretly developing lightning-fast tanks for the German army.

I sighed gloomily, but moments later my ears pricked up. Papa was trying to persuade my mother to come down for the weekend. I leaned forward, straining to hear if there was any sign it was working.

"Bertrand and Christian are coming down tomorrow," he told her. "You could hitch a lift with them and arrive in style. Then you could take Angelo back."

My heart suddenly clenched. Going home was the last thing I wanted. For a start, it might mean being sent back to school. But more importantly, I hadn't made things right yet. Ever since I'd crushed my father's car—not to mention his career—I'd vowed I would do everything in my power to make up for it. I didn't know how . . . just that I had to try.

I headed outside, feeling more despondent than ever, and soon found myself back at the rickety old garage. As I lifted the latch, a bird fluttered up in my face and flew out through a hole in the roof. The shock made me bark my shin against the broken shaft of an old pitchfork, and I cursed in my best slang. If only Maman could hear what I'd been learning at my fancy school! The thought cheered me a little, and as my eyes grew accustomed to the light, I decided to explore a little further.

Behind the tractor the shed was crammed to the roof with rusty old gardening tools and tin cans—debris that seemed to have lain untouched for tens of years. As I pulled at some wooden crates, I caught a glimpse of something bulky lurking at the back under an old tarpaulin. Clambering over the junk, I gave it several sharp tugs—until all at once it slid off, sending up a thick cloud of dust that made me double up coughing.

When my eyes finally stopped streaming, I realized that I was staring at another vehicle of some sort. I'd seen something similar in my father's studio once: an aging photograph, peeling at the corners, that showed one of the earliest motorcars from the turn of the century.

Using my sleeve, I began to wipe away the dust on the door, and then my eyes suddenly widened like saucers. Two white lines had emerged in the shape of a faded cross.

It was an old ambulance—possibly from the Great War, twenty years ago. The front of the vehicle—the bonnet and driver's cabin—looked like a very grand (if dusty) vintage car. But a large wooden box had been attached to the back, presumably where the stretchers were stowed.

I tugged the door open and climbed up into the cabin. But as I slid in behind the steering wheel, I failed to see a large spring that had burst through the upholstery. No sooner had I sat on it than I leaped up with a yelp, clonking my head on the ceiling and ripping a hole clean through the seat of my trousers.

Brilliant! Another reason for my mother to give me an earful. I groaned, peering round at my rear end.

When my head had finally stopped throbbing, I turned to discover a moldy curtain separating the cabin from the wooden box at the back. A little more cautious this time, I drew it back and peered into the gloom beyond.

Inside, there were two canvas stretchers suspended from the ceiling like hammocks. But it was what lay beside them that really caught my eye. On the floor, caked in a thick layer of dust, was an antique gas mask. I stretched out my fingers hungrily and pulled it over by the strap. Little more than a pair of goggles, it had a piece of cloth folded into a pad—presumably to filter mustard gas in the trenches.

Suddenly a voice behind me made me spin round.

"What are you doing in here?" The girl was standing in the doorway, staring at me accusingly.

Guiltily, I let the gas mask drop and cleared my throat. "I found the door open, so—"

"Monsieur Hipaux doesn't like anybody poking around. You have to leave," she said sharply.

"Why?" I asked, frowning. "I'm not doing any harm. Anyway, I'm good with old cars and things."

The girl raised an eyebrow. "Somehow I doubt that." She was obviously referring to the earlier incident with the lawn mower. "Now please leave."

Grudgingly, I made my way outside and watched her lock the door with a large rusty key. "Where did the ambulance come from anyway?" I asked.

"Nosy, aren't you?" she said, before stowing the key inside her shawl and turning to leave.

"Wait. Where are you going?"

She stopped and eyed me suspiciously again. "Why?"

"If you're going to get food, I could help," I mumbled. "It's not like there's anything else to do."

"Thanks, but I don't need any help," she said gruffly. With that, she turned and stalked off across the courtyard.

"Couldn't you at least show me round . . . ?" I called after her, but either she couldn't hear me or she chose not to.

Fine, I thought. *If she doesn't want to be my guide, I'll just follow her instead.* So no sooner had she disappeared through the gates than I set off after her.

For a while I kept pace about twenty meters behind, ducking behind a tree whenever I thought she might turn and see me. When we reached the village, I saw her take a left turn, away from the bar, before climbing some steps. Curious to know where she was heading, I carried on shadowing her. But by the time I reached the top of the steps, she was nowhere to be seen. Instead, a mangy old tomcat with only one eye jerked its head to look at me, then scurried off through the snow.

"Shoot," I muttered under my breath: she'd given me the slip. Not knowing which way to turn, I decided to follow what looked like a fresh set of footprints in the snow. The track ahead led back down to the square by way of a large loop, and it wasn't long before I came to an area of wasteland with a rusty old petrol pump. Beyond it were the doors to what appeared to be the local smithy. I wiped vigorously at the glass and tried to peer in, but it was too ingrained with dirt to see more than a half meter or so inside.

With a last glance around, I sighed with frustration and headed back toward the manor house.

She had beaten me . . . for now.

6 Julietta Arrives

The following day my mother came to join us. She, Bertrand and Christian drove down from Paris in Christian's latest toy—a canary-yellow BMW roadster that was all chrome running boards, shiny headlamps and dimpled leather upholstery. Christian never drove anything that wasn't the latest model of something, and this was no exception.

Splashing through the mud and melting snow, the car couldn't have looked more exotic as it swept in through the gates to the manor house and crunched to a halt in front of us.

Taking Bertrand's hand, my mother stepped regally from the car, only for her expression to falter. I knew straightaway what she was thinking. This was Uncle Bertrand's château? It looked more like a dilapidated ruin. But as soon as she saw me, her face broke into a smile. She hugged me to her, squeezing me till I thought my eyes would pop.

"Maman . . . !" I gasped as she was about to suffocate me. She let me go and stepped back to take a look at what I was wearing. I had found some work clothes in the cellar—coveralls and cap that made me feel like I was back in my father's workshop. It had the added benefit of hiding the large rip in the seat of my corduroy trousers.

"You look like a mechanic." She grimaced, staring at me.

"I want to be a mechanic," I protested, and she rolled her eyes.

"I suppose it's an improvement on street urchin."

"I think he looks entirely the part," Bertrand declared, studying me evenly. "And I'm especially fond of street urchins. I find they make the very best stew, though they can be a little gristly."

"I found the old garage," I told him enthusiastically. "There's even an ancient ambulance."

"Ah, that old thing." Bertrand beamed, his eyes dancing with boyish excitement. "You know it was originally a Rolls-Royce? Well, at least the front end."

My mother look astonished. "They turned a Rolls-Royce into an ambulance? Whatever for?"

"I would have thought that was obvious, my dear," Bertrand said, glancing over his glasses. "To save people's lives."

Maman smiled uneasily as Christian grabbed the suitcases and threw them to my father.

"Bit grim," he said, eyeing the house. "Reminds me of one of the dumps I used to run away from as a child." He lit one of his exotic foreign cigarettes and put an arm round me as we headed in. "So, young Angelo, I want to hear all about the local women."

"Christian!" my mother tutted, pretending to be shocked, though I suspected she was secretly thrilled by his roguishness.

At dinner my mother forced me to wear the jacket and trousers she had brought down from Paris. I sat opposite her, scratching my neck where the jacket rubbed my skin and scowling sulkily. I'd been looking forward to her coming all day, hoping against hope that a spell in the countryside would be exactly what my parents needed to make them get on again. But now that she was here, I realized it was a terrible mistake. From the moment she'd stepped out of the car, it was obvious that she would hate it.

The young housemaid came in and began ladling some kind of thin vegetable gruel into our bowls. As she finished serving me, I realized Christian was watching me with a wry glint in his eye.

"You young rascal!" he teased with a playful nudge. "You've got your eye on her, haven't you?"

Seeing she'd overheard, I felt my face start to burn with embarrassment. Luckily, Bertrand was on hand to rescue me.

"I hear the delivery van broke down again. I hope you didn't both starve."

"Not at all." I smiled, brightening. "In fact, we took the lawn mower into the village."

"Lawn mower?" Christian spluttered, nearly choking on his gruel. He turned and gave my father a mischievous scowl. "I hope this isn't some new prototype you've been working on without me, you sly dog."

Papa smiled, but I could see that the joke was a little too close to the bone.

"Now you mention it, I couldn't help noticing a lack of motorcars in the village," my mother added. She turned to Bertrand playfully. "Have you banned the locals from owning them?"

He wiped his mouth carefully before answering. "The average income in Regnac doesn't quite stretch to luxury sports cars, my dear. Not that that's stopped Victor from trying to make a case for an official vehicle."

"Who's Victor?" Maman asked curiously.

"He runs the local bar."

"So why does he need an official vehicle?" Christian asked.

"Because he also happens to be Regnac's mayor," Bertrand explained.

"Mayor?" My father gulped. "No wonder the place is going to the wall."

I saw a flicker of irritation cross Bertrand's face. "What makes you say that?"

"Let's just say we had a little run-in with him yesterday." My father sniffed. "He didn't exactly welcome us with open arms."

"No wonder," my mother said, "if you turned up on a lawn mower."

After dinner, while my father, Bertrand and Christian stepped outside onto the gravel to smoke, I decided to give my mother the slip. I knew she would only make me take a bath in the freezing mausoleum that pretended to be a bathroom. Then she would run the nit comb through my hair. Since her arrival she had become convinced that the house was infested with lice and fleas. Which, in fairness, it probably was.

Instead, I decided to lie low in the flagstoned cellar. It might be several hours before my mother abandoned her search for me, so I found myself an old crate in the corner and settled down to doodle car designs.

Just above me, a grille opened out at ground level. Through it, I could hear my father and the others as they smoked and chatted.

Suddenly I sat rigid. The young housemaid had entered the cellar.

Frozen to the spot, I watched as she emptied the dregs of the wine from supper into a dusty old bottle.

"Tell me," I heard Papa asking above. "Has Marguerite always been mute?"

"Not at all," Bertrand replied. "She just chooses not to speak."

"I thought she just disliked me," my father grunted.

"She hasn't said a word since her baby was delivered stillborn over twenty years ago," Bertrand explained. "Must have been the shock. She's had another child since then—Amandine. But she still won't say anything. Not a single word."

"The serving girl doesn't say much either," Christian complained, sucking on one of his foreign cigarettes again. "What's her name?"

"Camille," Bertrand answered. "She's probably just suspicious of you. You can hardly blame her."

Camille immediately stopped pouring the wine. Realizing

that they were talking about her, she tilted her head to listen. In the moonlight I could see the way her dark eyebrows framed guarded, watchful eyes. A second later her eyes adjusted a fraction and suddenly she was staring straight at me.

She sprang back and stared at me defiantly. "Are you spying on me?"

"N-no," I stammered. "I promise. I was trying to hide from my mother."

And as if summoned by my words, Maman now stepped out to join the others above. "Have you seen Angelo?" she demanded sharply.

Down below, I shook my head imploringly at Camille. "Please . . ."

I was certain she was going to give me away, but to my surprise she said nothing.

"I'm sure you can afford to relax the reins a little," I heard Bertrand suggest soothingly. "After all, he is on holiday."

Camille gave me one of her withering looks, then turned abruptly and stalked out of the cellar.

As I watched her march up the stairs, I realized two things with absolute certainty.

The first was that I would become firm friends with her. The second was that right now, she hated my guts.

7 The Test Track

I sat shivering in the steel tub while my mother barked orders at me from the other side of the bathroom door. I'd managed to avoid her the previous night, but she'd finally caught up with me after breakfast and forced me to take a bath. Halfway through filling the tub, the water suddenly turned brown, so I was now huddling in only a few inches of tepid, rust-colored water.

I could tell that Maman had something important she wanted to say.

"Angelo?" she ventured timidly from the landing outside.

At first I didn't answer. Apart from anything else, my teeth were chattering from the cold.

"Please answer me, dear."

"What?" I replied sulkily.

"I know you're angry—about your father and me . . . taking time apart. And that's OK. I don't blame you. But you have to understand, this is nothing to do with you. . . ." She sounded flustered now, babbling a little. "I mean, you mustn't ever think it's your fault. However things turn out, we will always love you, so very much. You do know that, don't you?" She suddenly fell silent, waiting patiently for my answer. "Angelo . . . ?"

Inside the bathroom, I'd stopped shivering. I sat quite still, refusing to give my mother the reassurance she so desperately wanted.

I knew that it was cruel of me to punish her, that I should have told her I understood that sometimes people fall out of love. This was what the rational side of my brain kept telling me. But I didn't want to be rational. I was furious. Hadn't she promised she would love my father for richer and for poorer?

I gritted my teeth and forced myself not to say anything. For a moment my mother was silent as well, and I wondered if she was crying.

"Maybe we could take a trip to see Grandpapa back in Italy. You'd like that, wouldn't you?" Her voice sounded desperate now, but going on holiday to Italy was the last thing I wanted to do. I wanted to be here, making things right again.

Getting no response, my mother finally gave up. "Don't be too long," she whispered, her voice catching with emotion. Then I heard her footsteps echo away.

I felt a sharp pang of guilt. I squeezed my eyes shut as tightly as I could to block out the hurt, then leaped out of the bath.

A few hours later, we were all squeezed like sardines into Christian's sports car. Despite the freezing weather, he thought it would be exhilarating to roll the roof down. So I was now sandwiched in the back between Bertrand and my mother, who was swathed in a huge scarf, while Christian sat in the front with my father.

"You still haven't said where we're going," Maman protested, her voice muffled behind layers of scarf.

"To the test track," Bertrand roared above the noise of the wind and the engine.

"Test track?" I repeated, my spirits suddenly soaring. "Here?"

"Didn't you know? It's where our first-ever models were tried out."

I stood up to peer around for any sign of it, only for my mother to yank me back down.

"For goodness' sake, Angelo, you'll get yourself killed," she scolded. "Besides, you should show a little more decorum."

Decorum was a word Maman often used. I still didn't know what it meant, even less how to show it.

By now the weather had become spiteful, stinging our faces with gusts of horizontal sleet. After one particularly cruel blast, my mother's scarf blew clean off and stuck itself to the windshield.

Suddenly blinded, Christian swerved, only just missing a cow that was standing in the middle of the lane. As the car veered toward the hedge, the front wheels leaped over the grass verge and sank into a boggy ditch.

"Blast it!" he cursed, leaping out to assess the damage.

"If it's OK," my mother announced a little shakily, "I think I'd like to go home now."

Christian's disembodied voice echoed from behind the radiator. "That may not be as easy as you think. The tire's flat."

Bertrand, however, was already out. "Not to worry. We've arrived."

I frowned and looked around. Arrived? "But this is just a field."

"To the untrained eye, perhaps." He winked. "Come on, it's still a little walk from here."

As I jumped down, my feet immediately sank into ten centimeters of icy mud, and my mother's face turned even paler.

"If it's all the same, I think I'll stay," she declared.

The ever-thoughtful Bertrand took the large blanket out of the back and laid it over her lap. "There," he said. "That should keep you warm. We won't be long."

And with that we four men—or should I say three and a half men?—strode out across the soaking grass, leaving Maman with just the cow for company.

The test track itself lay another two and a half fields away. When we finally reached it, nobody said a word for nearly a minute. Apart from anything else, no one except Bertrand could be sure what we were supposed to be looking at.

To all appearances, we were standing at the edge of yet another dreary field. But when I peered more closely at the ground, I saw something poking up through the snow and weeds. Fragments of crumbling tarmac.

"This is it," Bertrand whispered, a boyish grin lighting

up his face. "This is where I tested our first successful model when I was a lad."

"No wonder it's so overgrown, if it was that long ago." Christian snorted wryly.

Bertrand ignored him and turned to my father, his eyes glistening. "I don't care what the Money Men say. One day you're going to design a car that I can test here again. Something France has never seen before. You've done it before and you're going to do it again."

Papa glanced around uncertainly. "Surely the only thing you can test here is a tractor?"

"Maybe that's what he had in mind," Christian joked. He hadn't meant anything by it—he never did—but by now my father had heard enough jokes at his own expense.

"I better check on Julietta." He scowled, and began the muddy trudge back to the car.

Bertrand watched him head away and sighed, heavy-hearted.

But if Papa was feeling downcast, Bertrand's words had given me a new shot of encouragement. If I could just persuade my father to try and create one more hit design, maybe everything could be saved: my father's career . . . even my parents' marriage.

I turned and looked up at Bertrand, my eyes gleaming with determination. "If he won't design you a car," I told him defiantly, "I will."

8 A Bridge Too Far

An hour later, with the spare tire finally in place, Christian steered our bright yellow sports car off the rutted lane and we began the tortuous journey back to Regnac.

No sooner had we swept our way up the hill and into the main square than there was a sudden squeal of rubber on wet cobbles and Bertrand, my mother and I were flung forward, our faces plastered against the seat in front.

When I looked up, I found myself gazing into the tired eyes of an old donkey, standing stock-still in front of us.

"What is it with the animals in this village!" Christian cursed, leaping out to shoo the old ass out of the way.

The donkey, however, had other ideas, resolutely refusing to budge. Despite Christian's best efforts, she simply blinked at him through her long eyelashes and thrashed her matted tail, then did absolutely nothing.

"It won't make any difference," Bertrand explained. "It's Geneviève—she belongs to the farmer, Benoît. You'll have to go round her."

"What's she doing standing here anyway?" Christian grumbled.

"Delivering the post," boomed a voice out of nowhere. "Or she should have been."

I glanced over and saw that the voice belonged to Victor, the bar owner—and, as we had now discovered, mayor.

"Why would a donkey be delivering the post?" I asked, baffled.

"Normally she wouldn't. But Marcel, the postman, slid on some ice and buckled his bicycle wheel. Now he's laid up at home with a twisted ankle."

An idea suddenly popped into my head and I tugged on Bertrand's arm. "Couldn't we deliver the post in the car?"

"What an excellent notion!" he agreed without batting an eyelid.

"Not so fast," Christian protested. "I for one have had more than enough wild-goose chases across bumpy lanes. Someone else can drive. Besides, one of us needs to escort Julietta back to the house."

"In that case, Luca can drive," Bertrand declared.

My father started to complain, but I quickly intervened. "Please, Papa—it would be an adventure."

He thought about arguing, then resigned himself. "Fine." He sighed. "But Bertrand will have to do the map-reading."

"Agreed," Bertrand said.

Fifteen minutes later, the post for the entire local district, in a variety of sacks, had been loaded into the back of Christian's sports car. With everything stowed, Victor appeared clutching two chickens, one under each arm, and handed them to me.

"Make sure you give them to Jean-Pierre," he growled. "Monsieur Hipaux will know where he lives. Tell him they're payment for fixing the table."

His words were drowned out by the rasping of gears as my father shunted the car abruptly into reverse.

Geneviève, who had remained rooted to the spot the whole time, marked the occasion with a loud bray and then deposited a toffee apple of dung within a hairsbreadth of my mother's elegant shoes.

I clung tightly to the sacks of post—and the chickens—as, with a jolt, my father swung the car out into the road.

"Technically, you're going the wrong way," Bertrand shouted across to him.

"You mean there's a right way?" Papa asked as he gripped the wheel. I couldn't be sure, but I thought he might just be starting to enjoy himself.

At the bottom of the road leading away from the village, we ground to a halt again and I tugged down my goggles to join my father and Bertrand as they peered over the bonnet.

Up ahead, the road looked like it had come under heavy enemy bombardment. Every meter or so there were craters brimming with muddy snow.

"There's nothing for it," Bertrand declared. "We'll have

to take the bridge. But you'll have to drive across the field to get to it." He nodded toward the field of corn stubble on our left.

At that moment I noticed a farmer and his wife approaching up the road. Peering more closely, I realized that the woman was Marguerite, the mute, granite-jawed housekeeper we'd met on our first night. Her husband, who I would soon learn went by the name of Benoît—owner of the donkey—was old and crooked, with all his teeth missing except for two nicotine-stained pegs that clung precariously to his gums. His few wisps of hair were stuffed under the rim of his beret.

Both of them were heavily laden. Benoît was carrying what turned out to be two earthenware pitchers of homemade wine, while Marguerite was balancing trays of freshly laid eggs, still covered in straw and bird muck. When they finally reached us, Benoît struck up a conversation with Bertrand in an accent so thick I decided it must be entirely made-up. At the end of it, Bertrand leaped out and began helping them into the back of the car.

"What are you doing?" my father asked, confused by this new turn of events.

"Their cart horse is lame," Bertrand explained. "We're giving them a lift to the market in Boutonne."

As Benoît and Marguerite clambered into the back with me, some of the wine slopped onto the leather upholstery and I winced at its rancid smell.

"You can't tell me he's planning to sell that stuff?" I whispered.

Bertrand looked surprised. "Sell it? Good heavens, no—that's what he drinks while he waits for Marguerite to sell the eggs."

I glanced at the old man, who grinned back amiably, one of his yellow pegs jutting out. A moment later my father swung the car left and we began to lurch our way across the field.

Ahead of us the earth was so frozen, the wheels of the car jolted and creaked as we bounced over the icy puddles. I eyed the tray of eggs that Marguerite was clutching on her lap. As we lurched over a particularly steep hump, one, quickly followed by another, leaped spontaneously off the tray, hit my father's neck and cracked. Egg white dripped down his nape.

"This is hopeless!" he cursed, dabbing at his sticky collar. However, Bertrand continued to smile throughout, clearly amused by the whole adventure.

After a painstaking ten minutes we finally arrived at the bridge.

The term *bridge* was a fairly loose one, as the bridge consisted of little more than a few rotten beams with some sheets of rusty metal laid across.

"I recommend you get a long run-up before you attempt it," Bertrand advised my father.

"You actually expect us to go over that?" he asked.

"How else are we going to deliver the post?" Bertrand replied. "Everyone ready?"

I wiped my goggles and gave the thumbs-up, while Benoît took a large swig of wine for courage.

Taking a deep breath, my father made the sign of the cross, then floored the pedal as hard as he could. As the car began its approach, Bertrand leaned across and shouted over the noise.

"If you could try not to break any more of her eggs, I'm sure Marguerite would be grateful."

"It's our necks I'm trying not to break," Papa shouted back.

In a matter of seconds the iron bridge rushed up and the front wheels connected. But as the car thundered onto the metal sheets, I heard the wooden structure start to groan, its timber supports complaining under the unexpected weight.

Suddenly the groaning was joined by another noise; something far more sinister. Eyes bulging, I realized that it was the sound of the woodwork starting to splinter. A second later a huge crack echoed out, then another. One by one, the wooden stanchions holding up the bridge were beginning to shear clean through.

A few seconds more, and we would have been across. My knuckles went white as my nails dug into the leather seat, willing the car forward.

The bridge was imploding in front of us. The only thing still carrying us forward was the sheer momentum of its collapse.

For a moment the car was teetering, suspended in midair, before its nose finally crunched into the snowy bank on the other side.

My father's foot pressed frantically against the metal of the footwell as he urged the car up the icy slope. But it was no use. The wheels spun hopelessly, churning up the mud.

"Out, all of you! Quickly!" he cried, yanking on the handbrake.

I leaped over the side of the car, clutching both chickens, while Bertrand and my father bundled the farmer and his wife out of the backseat. Abandoning the tray of broken eggs, we scrambled up the slope and turned, panting, to survey the car, marooned behind us.

As we watched, powerless, it slid back into the stream, before finally coming to rest on the bottom, the freezing water lapping over the tops of its doors.

"The post!" I spluttered. "We have to save it!"

But it was too late. Armfuls of the stuff were already floating freely down the river, joined by a little flotilla of broken eggshells.

9 The Postal Service Lives On

"So, who's for another sightseeing trip tomorrow?" Bertrand asked, trying to thaw the frosty atmosphere at dinner that evening.

"In what, exactly?" Christian asked a little petulantly. "You sank my last car."

Another gloomy silence descended on the room. I slurped my soup as quietly as I could, watching my mother dart another scornful sideways glance at Papa.

Bertrand, in her eyes, could do no wrong, but my father was an entirely different matter. Ever since we'd made it back after our disastrous attempt to deliver the post, Maman had been berating him for trying to drown me, as she claimed.

She finished her dinner and folded her napkin neatly. "I

for one will be going on only one trip tomorrow," she announced crisply. "Straight back to Paris."

Bertrand reached for his pipe again. "Well, I'll be sorry to see you go, my dear, but we'll be sure to take good care of Angelo."

My mother threw a stern look at him. "Angelo will be coming home with me."

My spoon landed in my bowl with a loud clank, splashing soup down the napkin tucked into my collar. "P-please," I stammered. "I—I can't go back." I turned pleadingly to Bertrand. "Can't I stay?"

My mother scowled at me. "To catch pneumonia or drown? It's out of the question."

But Bertrand put a gentle hand on her arm. "Let him stay a few days longer. I'll make sure he comes to no harm," he promised, before adding sheepishly: "No more harm."

She bristled before finally relenting. "Very well. But only until Sunday. Not a day longer." Then she marched out of the room and headed upstairs to pack her bags.

The following morning, Friday, I watched the porter load my mother's cases onto the train in Boutonne, twenty kilometers away. She and Christian were taking the first available service back to Paris. Victor had arranged for one of the town hall chauffeurs to ferry us to the station and back—no doubt to try and impress us, or at least Bertrand, whom he clearly revered.

As my mother stiffly kissed my father goodbye, I thought she looked sad, mournful almost. Usually she looked plain irritated, but this was different. I couldn't work out if it was because she knew there was no hope now for their marriage—or whether there was another reason.

The previous night, as I dawdled on my way up to bed, I'd heard Bertrand and Papa out on the gravel.

"Don't worry about Christian," Bertrand was saying. "I'll see to it he's given another sports car to make up for the one I lost him in the river. In the meantime I'll need to head back to Paris myself in the next day or so. The board have summoned me to another emergency meeting."

"To decide my fate?" my father asked gloomily.

"Actually, it's to decide what to do about the factory."

I suddenly froze. Surely the factory wasn't going to close as well? But as hard as I tried, I couldn't make out what Bertrand said next. It seemed to be something about the Germans, but for once it wasn't about Dr. Ferdinand Porsche. It was about Adolf Hitler, the German Chancellor. Before I could hear any more, Maman found me on the stairs and shooed me off to bed.

Now, standing on the platform as she was about to leave, I couldn't shake the feeling that what my father had been whispering about had something to do with my mother's sad expression.

I watched her hold out her hand delicately for Bertrand to kiss, but he brushed it aside and caught her up in his long arms, all but knocking her hat off. It struck me suddenly how young she looked again, almost vulnerable. Then she turned to me and I braced myself for a lecture on how to dress appropriately.

To my surprise, it didn't come. Instead she clasped me to

her and kissed me wetly on the cheek in a way she hadn't since I was a small boy. When she looked at me, her eyes were glistening with tears. In that moment I realized she was more than just sad to leave me. She was frightened.

"Be careful. No more postal deliveries," she said, before adding, "And enjoy yourself."

I was suddenly thrown. It was the first time she'd ever said anything like that. She was always on at me to work harder, to behave with more decorum.

Christian was now gripping my father's hand vigorously. "Next time I see you we may be designing tanks."

"Never," my father retorted proudly. "Christian Silvestre and Luca Fabrizzi will only ever create works of engineering genius for beautiful people."

Christian jumped aboard and joined my mother at the window as the train pulled out.

As I waved goodbye, I had the strange sensation that nothing would ever be quite the same again. Things had changed already—the very fact that Maman had allowed me to stay behind without her—but something else was nagging at me.

I turned to Papa. "What did Christian mean about designing tanks? Has it got something to do with the factory?"

For a moment he looked awkward.

"Nothing." He shrugged. "Just a joke."

❈

A little later I sat with him and Bertrand in Victor's bar, staring out at the half-melted snow. Dominique, Victor's wife, emerged from the back with our drinks. Slim as a reed, with her long auburn hair tied securely, she was wearing a plain, muted dress with a baggy cardigan pulled round her, almost as if she wanted to cover up as much of herself as she could.

As she brought our drinks to the table, I wondered if she'd picked up on our glum mood, because she slipped a small plate of almond macaroons onto the table.

My father's eyes lit up with delight. "I see the delivery van has been repaired."

"Oh, these aren't from Boutonne," Bertrand corrected as he cleaned his glasses for the umpteenth time that morning. "Dominique makes them herself. She's quite the expert confectioner. You should try her praline truffles."

My father and I exchanged a look of astonishment before falling upon the macaroons greedily. As the almond crust crumbled in my mouth, I felt the gooey center melt like butter on my tongue.

I could tell that Papa was thinking the same as me: was it possible they were even more delicious than the ones from the pâtisserie across the road from the factory?

We'd hardly had time to savor our macaroons before Victor was making a beeline for our table.

"I trust you are enjoying the little amuse-bouches I sent over," he said, nodding to the crumbs on the plate.

Bertrand smiled back. "It's only a shame we won't be staying long enough to enjoy more of Dominique's creations."

"Ah," Victor sighed, with a glint of amusement in his eye. "So you won't be delivering the post on a regular basis?"

I saw my father's jaw tighten at what he took to be a sly dig, but Bertrand was quick to keep things amiable.

"So you heard about our little adventure with the bridge?"

"I'm afraid the whole village is talking about it." Victor smirked. "I believe some of the mail even washed up in Bordeaux. Perhaps we should float it down there more often," he quipped, before heading back to the bar.

"Ignore him," Bertrand urged my father, seeing him bristle. "I told you, he means no real harm."

"But what about tomorrow's post?" I asked. "How will it be delivered if the postman's bike is broken and the donkey refuses to budge?"

"They could always use the lawn mower," Papa replied.

"Of course!" I cried, seizing on the idea. "We could fix some kind of trailer behind it. Then we could give the farmer and his wife a lift as well."

"What they really need's a tank," my father grunted unhelpfully. "Mind you, there should be a few of those before long."

This time I wasn't going to be fobbed off so easily. "Why do you keep talking about tanks?" I demanded.

My father and Bertrand exchanged an awkward glance before Bertrand cleared his throat uneasily.

"What your father isn't telling you is that there may be a war."

I went cold.

"It may never happen," Bertrand reassured me, but I could see that Papa wasn't so sure.

"Will you have to fight?" I asked him warily. "If it comes to it?"

"It depends whether the French want me to. If the Italians side with Hitler, I could be the enemy," he answered darkly.

Before I could ask any more questions, a young lad of about sixteen entered the café carrying a large school satchel. He was broad and physically strong, his muscular arms squeezed into school clothes that he'd long outgrown. Victor greeted him warmly, slapping him on the shoulder, then brought him over to meet us.

"Monsieur Hipaux, you'll remember my son, Philippe?" he said proudly.

"Of course." Bertrand smiled and shook the boy's hand. "Though it's been a few years. You've grown."

"Philippe is studying to be an engineer. Perhaps you'll want to employ him in your factory one of these days?"

"You should all come up to the house for dinner, and Philippe can tell me all about his studies," Bertrand suggested, out of politeness.

But Victor's eyes lit up immediately. "We'd be delighted," he said, turning to Philippe. "Wouldn't we?"

Philippe nodded curtly without smiling. Clearly the idea didn't excite him. I couldn't pretend I was looking forward to it much either.

⚙

Dinner that evening never seemed to end. Victor droned on interminably about all his ambitions for Philippe. If war broke out, his son's career would be best served in the engineering corps or logistics, he insisted: somewhere that would further his prospects once any possible conflict was over.

Philippe, however, had other ideas.

"I don't want to further my career," he said with a scowl

in a rare moment of defiance. "I want to serve my country by joining the air corps."

"Nonsense," Dominique reprimanded him gently. "You're far too young for talk about signing up."

Now that the conversation had come round to flying machines, I began to wake up.

"Didn't you fly for the air corps during the war?" I asked Bertrand.

"Monsieur Hipaux won no less than the Military Cross," Victor announced loftily—a fact I was already aware of since Bertrand had let me look after his medal in my top drawer at home. "But I'm sure you'd agree," he went on, "that your career would have been far better served had there never been a war." He looked to Bertrand for support, but he wasn't about to get it.

"Actually, I think it was essential. It taught me to take risks. Which is something no formal training can teach you."

"I suppose Monsieur Fabrizzi here had no formal training either?" Victor asked with a hint of sarcasm, glancing across at my father. "Sorry, Signor Fabrizzi," he corrected. I wondered if he was making some sly dig about my father being Italian.

Papa smiled coolly. "I prefer *Monsieur,*" he replied evenly. "And for the record, no, I have almost no formal qualifications whatsoever."

Victor gave a loud snort. "You expect us to believe Monsieur Hipaux hired you to design luxury cars with no experience?"

"That's exactly what I did!" Bertrand exclaimed. "When I first came across Luca's work I thought it showed such

flair—such a rare gift—that I employed him on the spot."
He smiled at my father. "I've never once regretted my decision."

There was an awkward silence, during which Camille
came in to clear the dishes. Bertrand complimented her on
the soup, but Victor showed no such grace, belching through
his ferrety whiskers.

As Camille took the last of the plates, I became aware
of Philippe's eyes following her every movement. A few
moments after she left the room, he excused himself and
slipped out too.

"So," Victor continued, a little sulkily now, "have you
come to Regnac to work on a new design?"

"Actually, I came here to get away from designing cars,"
my father replied.

"After your experience down by the river, maybe you
should try your hand at building a boat."

Seeing Papa's volcanic temper about to erupt, I blurted
out the first thing that came into my head.

"I've got a much better idea."

"Let me guess," Victor said with a sniff. "A new postal
van."

"Yes," I replied, which seemed to take him by surprise.
"But not just a postal van. A car that ordinary people can
drive."

As the words left my mouth, I realized that the idea had
secretly been going around inside my head ever since the
accident on the bridge. Now, suddenly, it seemed blindingly
obvious.

My father, however, was looking unimpressed. "You think

they want one after today?" he scoffed. "I suspect they'll be too busy laughing at the last one we parked in their river."

"But it was the wrong design," I persisted. "It was too heavy, and the wheels were too hard. If the suspension was softer, like your last design—"

"My last design is the reason we're sitting here now," Papa snapped, pushing his chair back as if to leave the table.

But Bertrand put a gentle hand on his arm to stop him. "At least hear Angelo out. He may have a point."

My father sighed and sank back into his seat as Bertrand nodded at me to continue.

"In the field—I mean, the test track," I stuttered. "You said you wanted a car that France had never seen before. Something entirely new."

"I did," he replied uncertainly.

"Well, can't you see?" I asked, turning to my father urgently. "This could be it."

"And who exactly would buy this car?" he asked. "People like that old farmer, Benoît?"

"Yes," I cried, warming to my theme now. "If it was cheap enough."

At that Victor guffawed. "Better make it simple enough for his wife to drive, then. Because he spends most of his time in my bar."

"Perhaps Marguerite would like to drive it," Dominique suddenly chimed in. "I know I would." She'd been so quiet all evening, I'd almost forgotten she was there (probably because Victor hadn't stopped gassing on). But now that I looked at her, she seemed different. Her soft hazel eyes, which she normally kept averted, were suddenly gleaming in the candlelight.

Victor clearly didn't share her newfound enthusiasm and harrumphed grumpily.

I turned urgently to Papa. "Please," I pleaded. "At least think about it. All people have ever done before is build cars for rich people in the cities. But what about everyone else? Why do they have to ride around on donkeys like something out of the Middle Ages?"

"Because most of them are too poor to afford a car," Victor told me. "Besides, have you seen the state of our roads?"

"Then we have to design a car with better suspension," I insisted. "One that can drive over a plowed field without breaking eggs or spilling wine."

Victor nearly choked on his drink. "If you manage that, they'll call you a miracle worker. We'll have flocks of pilgrims coming to pay homage to you!"

A wry smile played on Bertrand's lips. "You think it can't be done?" he asked.

"I think your little adventure on the bridge proved it," Victor replied.

"Well, there you are, Angelo," Bertrand said, winking at me. "You will have to prove the mayor wrong."

I suddenly realized that I'd got so carried away with my new idea, I'd completely forgotten about Philippe and Camille. Something about the way he'd pursued her out of the room had made me uneasy. I quickly excused myself, saying I needed an early night if I was going to start work on my design. Then I hurried out.

To my surprise, there was no sign of either of them in the kitchen. Confused, I headed back into the hallway, only to hear whispering coming from the cellar.

I made my way cautiously down the steps, my eyes slowly growing used to the gloom. When I finally stepped through the doorway, my skin burned like I'd been scalded.

Philippe and Camille were talking, but he was standing uncomfortably close to her, and his arm was barring the doorway so that she couldn't leave the room. She was trying to push past him, but he refused to budge.

Suddenly Camille saw me watching and landed a sharp kick on Philippe's shin.

Philippe winced, then turned and saw me. "What?" he asked balefully.

"I don't think she wants to talk to you," I said, trying to keep my voice steady.

He took a step toward me, bristling with menace. "Really? And who says?"

I stared up at him. He was a good ten centimeters taller than me and built like a brick outhouse, not a skinny whelp. I could see his flexed biceps straining against his shirt sleeves.

Camille quickly stepped between us. "Thank you, but I don't need your help. Philippe is just going," she said, staring at him defiantly.

Philippe's eyes drilled into mine in an unspoken threat; then he turned and stalked away.

I sighed with relief and my heart rate began to level out again. "I'm sorry, I—I didn't mean to intrude . . . ," I stammered.

Camille had whipped off her apron and was already putting on her coat. "I told you. I don't need your help. So stay out of my life!" she said, scowling. Then, without another word, she marched upstairs, her shoes echoing off the stonework. Moments later, I heard the side door creak on its hinges, then slam shut behind her. Through the grating above my head, I heard her tramp away through the snow.

Perhaps my confidence that we would become friends was misplaced after all.

10 Frankenstein's Monster

It was just after two o'clock the following day, Saturday, when Bertrand and my father looked up to see me standing in the doorway to the breakfast room. At first they hardly recognized me. I realized that my face must have been sprinkled with a fine layer of rust from where I'd patiently sawn away at the metal chair legs in the old ambulance.

"I thought you should know I've finished."

"Finished what?" my father asked.

"Come and see," I told him breathlessly.

Papa looked suspiciously at Bertrand. "Is this some nonsense you've put him up to?"

"Whatever gave you that idea?" he replied, feigning innocence.

A few moments later they were both standing outside, astonishment on their faces.

"What is it?" Papa asked cautiously.

I turned and surveyed the strange invention parked next to me. "It's my new prototype," I announced. "A car for ordinary people."

I had cobbled it together out of the lawn mower and a rusty old trailer I'd found hidden behind the tractor in the garage. Sitting on top were two canvas chairs I had borrowed from the ambulance.

Bertrand sucked on his pipe as he circled the bizarre contraption. "It doesn't have any suspension," he observed, but I was ready with my answer.

"The seats are heavily sprung, so they should absorb most of the impact of the potholes."

"What if it rains?" he asked.

"I've thought of that." I hauled an old canvas tent off the back of the trailer.

"All I need to do is tie this over the top. It won't protect against a storm, but it should at least be showerproof." I looked nervously at my father, who had yet to say anything. "What do you think?" I asked hopefully.

For a moment he looked completely lost for words. "It's very . . . unusual," he faltered. It wasn't exactly the overwhelming response I'd been hoping for.

"But can't you see?" I asked. "This could be your new design. I mean, obviously it needs a lot of restyling. . . ."

"Angelo, I know you're trying to help," he sighed wearily. "And I'm very grateful. But believe me, it's going to take a lot more than a battered old lawn mower with a couple of rusty seats to save my career."

"I admit it's a little rudimentary," Bertrand interrupted, "but don't be too quick to dismiss it. The boy might be on to something."

"Please, Papa," I protested. "At least let me demonstrate it for you."

"There's no point," my father replied, more sharply this time. "I told you, it won't make any difference."

"Surely there's no harm in letting him try . . . ," Bertrand reasoned.

Suddenly my father's temper boiled over. "We all need to stop kidding ourselves and face facts!" he snapped. "There isn't going to be a car, Angelo. Not this or any other one. Now put it all back where it came from and get your bags packed. We have to leave early in the morning." With that he turned and marched back inside.

I felt like I'd been thumped in the guts. It wasn't just that I'd spent so long making the prototype—it was that I really believed I was onto something. Sure, it looked stupid—but somewhere in amongst that pile of rusty metalwork and old cogs there was a dazzling new design just waiting to be discovered. I'd never been more certain of anything.

Bertrand must have seen how dejected I looked; he rested one of his long, knobbly hands on my shoulder. "Don't take it too hard. It's himself he's angry with, not you."

I felt hot tears start to well up in my eyes and had to look down before I betrayed myself.

Bertrand must have sensed it. "You know, you could always take this over to the blacksmith in the village," he suggested thoughtfully.

"What's the point?" I grumbled, kicking at the gravel tetchily.

"If you don't leave till the morning . . . that still gives you this afternoon."

"For what?" I asked, confused.

"To take it on its first test run, of course." I looked up and saw a twinkle of devilment in his eye.

"B-but you heard what my father said," I stammered.

"I did. But do you always do what your parents tell you?" he asked mischievously. With that, he patted me on the back and strolled back inside.

Less than an hour later, I was standing in the blacksmith's forge, the dusty little workshop I'd discovered the morning I'd followed Camille back to the village.

The blacksmith, Félix, was a tall, solid man of few words, with a bald head covered in soft gray down. His forearms were like the branches of an oak tree, while his face was deeply creased and careworn. As he came toward me, I noticed that he had a pronounced limp. Apparently a tractor he'd been welding once had toppled over and trapped his leg.

"Here," he grunted, offering me his spare mask.

"It's OK," I told him, pulling out the goggles I used in my father's workshop. "I brought my own."

In front of us sat my strange half–lawn mower, half-ambulance contraption. For the moment, the canvas seats had been hastily held in place with a few nails. But if the prototype was to stand any chance of completing its test run over a plowed field, Félix would need to weld them securely in place.

With the flick of a switch, his welding torch sparked into life and he set to work.

For the next thirty minutes I was in heaven again—back inside my father's workshop in Paris, the white-hot flame of the welding iron reflecting off my goggles.

Then, as suddenly as we had started, it was over. We raised our masks and peered at the ungainly creature in front of us.

"Will it hold?" I asked, eyeing the seats nervously.

Félix considered for a moment. Considering things earnestly was something he did a lot, I would discover. "That all depends. . . ."

"On what?"

"How big a bump you hit," he replied gruffly.

Suddenly a voice I knew all too well called from upstairs. "Papa . . . ?"

I spun round just in time to see Camille appear at the bottom of the stairs. So this was where she had disappeared the day I followed her. Félix must be her father.

"What are you doing here?" she asked, startled.

"Your father is doing . . . some work for me." I faltered, edging in front of the lawn mower. I was suddenly embarrassed by how absurd it looked. Curious, Camille stepped toward me and peered over my shoulder.

"What is it?" she asked uncertainly.

"I've made a sort of bet with Victor," I explained. "He

said I couldn't invent a vehicle that could drive across a field without breaking any eggs." I glanced between an astonished Camille and her father before adding sheepishly, "Or spilling any wine."

Camille looked at me like I was some kind of lunatic. "Without breaking any eggs?" she repeated. "This I've got to see."

11 The Maiden Voyage

Black clouds were building ominously as I swung the lawn mower through the gate into one of the lower fields not far from the village. Underfoot, or underwheel, the ground was roughly plowed, a series of deep furrows that gently sloped away, becoming steeper at the bottom, near the stream.

Camille walked behind me carrying a tray of eggs and a flagon of wine—everything we needed to conduct our first test run.

As we reached the top of the field, I lined the lawn mower up, facing slightly downhill to make things easier.

"If you'd like to take your seat," I said, nodding to one of the canvas hammocks.

Camille groaned, clearly wondering why she had ever agreed to this madcap experiment, then clambered aboard.

"Ready?" I asked, forcing a cautious smile.

"Why do I feel like I'm going to regret this?" she asked drily.

I took a deep breath to steady my nerves and eased out the choke so that the engine ran a little faster.

It was now or never.

I let out the clutch, and suddenly the machine bolted forward, nearly sending Camille toppling off behind. She hauled herself back on board and gripped the side of the seat, white-knuckled, as the lawn mower shuddered its way across the field.

At first I was scared that our combined weight might be too much: the lawn mower's engine was whining in protest. But gradually we began to pick up speed, gathering momentum as we approached the first frozen furrows in the field.

However, as we rattled over the stony ground, the seat I was perched on soon started to shudder. Out of the corner of my eye, I saw that the rivets Félix had welded onto the frame were already starting to crack.

I leaned forward, my goggles almost level with the handlebars as I willed the machine forward. But as we hit the first furrow, my chin crunched onto the metal, sending a shooting pain through my head that made my eyes water. Several eggs shot up out of their tray and would have smashed to the ground if Camille hadn't plucked them out of midair.

By now the field was starting to drop away more steeply, and I realized getting up enough speed was no longer the priority. It was stopping.

My heart started to race as I saw the danger looming ahead. Knowing that the brakes were hopeless, I shoved the choke in to try to slow the engine revs, only to find it made no difference. The lawn mower and its creaky chariot were by now almost in free fall down the hillside. Soon it was all I could do to hold on to the handlebars as we hit every bone-crunching pothole and gulley.

Behind me, Camille was holding on for dear life. Any attempt at protecting her precious cargo had been abandoned: eggs danced and then exploded into the air like firecrackers. With each stony hillock the trailer mounted, the wine flagon perched on her lap started to slide forward. Finally it slipped off and landed on the floor with a thump; the bottom of the jug sheared off and the wine went everywhere.

"You need to stop!" Camille shouted frantically.

"I can't!" I hollered back without turning my head. By now the bottom of the field was fast approaching and I knew I had to find a way to stop or we would soon be catapulted into the stream on the other side of the bank ahead. I thought of trying to swerve, but at this speed we would turn somersaults in the mud.

"We have to jump off!" I called back.

Camille glanced nervously at the frozen ground flying past. To leap would almost certainly be suicide. Suddenly there was a loud crack and the undercarriage of our seats broke clean away from the trailer. There was no longer anything keeping Camille attached to her chariot.

My stomach lurched as I realized that within seconds we would be in the river. Quite apart from the risk to life and limb, the idea of sinking two vehicles in as many days was unthinkable!

I needn't have worried. As we hit the last plowed furrow,

Camille was suddenly catapulted into the air as surely as if I'd pressed an ejector button. She landed with an awkward thump that made her cry out in pain before rolling over face-first in the mud.

At the last second, just as the lawn mower careered toward the riverbank, I leaped to safety.

I looked up just in time to see my crazy invention veer off into a tree and dismantle itself with a sickening crunch.

To my amazement, I was still in one piece. Battered and bruised and caked in freezing mud, yes, but otherwise unscathed. But it was only when I heard a groan behind me that I discovered Camille hadn't been so lucky. She was sitting in a muddy hollow, clutching her ankle in agony.

"Are you OK?" I gasped, rushing back to help her.

"Of course I'm not, you idiot!" she snarled, wincing in pain. "I think you've broken it."

Ten minutes later I finally staggered into the square, my boots clogged with heavy clay. The exertion of carrying Camille all the way up the hill had made my lungs burn, and I was certain I was about to be sick. But I knew my only hope of redeeming something from this disaster was to get her to a doctor as fast as my legs could carry her.

Victor's wife, Dominique, saw me first and came rushing out to help, quickly followed by Félix. He and Victor lifted Camille off my back and carried her into the café, while I collapsed onto a seat outside, retching from exhaustion.

A few minutes later, through the doorway, I saw Victor hang up the receiver of the old black Bakelite pay phone.

"Please," I asked falteringly. "How is she?"

"We won't know for sure till the doctor gets here from

Boutonne." He scowled. "What on earth were you doing out there?"

"It was the new design we were talking about," I muttered. "We were testing it and it . . ." I trailed off, too ashamed to admit the full story.

He looked at me and shook his head, disgusted. "I suppose it's something you didn't drown her, at least."

It was about ten minutes later that I finally saw my father striding across the square, accompanied by Bertrand.

"Is it true?" he hissed, his eyes blazing. "You deliberately defied me and now Camille has been injured?"

"Luca, please," Bertrand protested. "If you want to blâme someone, blame me."

But Papa wasn't listening. His jet-black eyes were drilling into me with scorn. "After what happened at the motor show, I thought you might have learned something. But you willfully persisted with this idiotic scheme. Well, I hope you're satisfied."

I looked at my feet, utterly ashamed. Just then the café door flew open and Félix emerged.

"How is she?" I asked, glancing up anxiously.

"This is Camille's father," Bertrand explained to my father.

"I am so sorry for my son's idiotic behavior," Papa began, but Félix held a hand up to stop him.

"The fault is mine," Félix grunted. "If I had welded the seat properly, Camille would never have fallen off." I couldn't believe what I was hearing—and nor, clearly, could my father. "Camille's ankle is fine," he assured me. "Sprained, nothing more. Now if you'll excuse me, I'm going to help her home." He nodded to my father, then headed back inside.

I let out a sigh as I felt the knot of tension start to unravel in my guts.

"So," Bertrand announced brightly. "No long-term harm caused after all."

But Papa was having none of it.

"You're lucky," he told me, simmering. "But this doesn't change anything. Go and pack your things."

Before I could mumble another apology, he was striding back across the square.

Bertrand took his pipe out of his pocket, stuffed it with several pinches of tobacco, then lit it. The tobacco glowed orange in the growing darkness as he sucked several mouthfuls into his cheeks.

"I'm so sorry . . . ," I began. "The test-drive was a complete disaster."

"Nonsense," Bertrand declared. "You have very successfully proved how not to design your car."

"I did that, all right," I moaned.

"Surely you didn't expect to get it right first go?" Bertrand exclaimed. "Even your father wouldn't be so arrogant as to presume that!"

"What use is it now anyway?" I grumbled. "You heard him. I'm going home tomorrow."

"You forget . . ." Bertrand smiled mysteriously. "Some things aren't meant to be. The rest aren't meant to be yet."

Dinner that night was eaten in complete silence. It was pointless trying to apologize any more to my father—he'd made it perfectly clear that he had nothing further to say.

So as soon as I'd finished my food, I excused myself from the table and left the room despondently.

As I closed the door, I hovered outside, hoping that my wounded silence might persuade him to have a change of heart. But I didn't hold out much hope. I knew how stubborn Papa could be once he'd set his mind on something. Especially when he was in a furious mood like this.

I leaned my ear against the paneled door and listened closely.

At first there was silence. I imagined Bertrand trying to fill his pipe or clean his spectacles again.

"It's funny," I heard him say after a moment.

"What?" my father grunted.

"Today I saw someone willing to take risks," he continued. "Willing to make a fool of himself for something he truly believed in. The only thing is, it wasn't you. It was Angelo."

My eyes bulged wider and I leaned in closer to hear how my father would react.

"The difference is that Angelo took risks with somebody else's life," he replied sharply. "He could have killed the girl."

"Are you sure that's what this is really about?"

"What does that mean?" Papa retorted.

"I mean, are you sure you aren't more concerned about losing face with Victor?"

"Don't be ridiculous! You think I care what that puffed-up buffoon thinks?"

"Yes," Bertrand replied. "I think you do. I think it's your own puffed-up ego that can't take it, not his."

For a moment there was silence. On the other side of the

door, I imagined my father's face flushing hot with fury. But when he finally spoke, his voice was calm.

"If you must know, this place is suffocating me."

"Because it reminds you of your own home back in Italy?" Bertrand suggested.

"Yes," my father admitted. I knew he'd always hated the village where he grew up.

"You know what impressed me the most when I first met you?" Bertrand asked after a moment. "That you didn't care what anyone else thought. You threw caution to the wind—invented fantastical cars the world had never seen—"

"And look where that got us!" my father snarled. "I won't make a fool of myself like that again. Not for anyone."

"So instead you live your life in fear?" Bertrand snorted. "Fear of failure. Fear of losing everything you had . . . of disappointing Julietta . . ."

I froze on the spot. Just as my father was no doubt doing at that very second.

"Angelo helped you create a masterpiece at the Paris Motor Show," Bertrand continued. "It may not have been successful, but that was because it was ahead of its time."

I was still holding my breath, barely daring to imagine what he was going to say next.

"Why not let him help you again?"

"You're actually serious about this car?" my father asked, incredulous.

"For Pete's sake, man, here at last is the chance to create something truly new. Something no one has done before—"

"To build a lawn mower for a farmer to sit on?" my father mocked.

"Yes!" Bertrand exclaimed, and I heard him thump the table. "Don't you see, Luca? The boy really is on to something. And if we don't do this now, the Germans will beat us to it. It's no secret that they're already developing a 'people's car' of their own."

"But who would buy it?" my father scoffed. "People like Benoît? Marguerite?"

"Yes!" Bertrand cried. "If it was cheap enough. Angelo is right," he went on. "France is living in the Dark Ages. But you could change all that, if you weren't too doggone proud to see it!" I couldn't remember the last time I'd heard him so passionate. "If you won't do it for me, at least do it for Angelo."

"For Angelo?" I heard my father utter in amazement.

"Are you really so blind?" Bertrand asked. "The boy's doing this for you."

I don't know what my father said after that, because I quickly brushed the tears from my cheeks and headed upstairs to bed.

12 The Crossroads

The following morning broke with an eerie stillness. It hadn't snowed for several days, and what was left on the ground was now slushy and brown.

By the time I stepped out into the half-light of dawn, my father was already warming up the motorbike in the yard. Bertrand was standing nearby, waiting for me. He forced a smile when he saw me approaching, but I wasn't fooled. I could tell he was as disappointed as I was that we were leaving—possibly more.

"Can I come back again soon?" I asked dismally, peering out from the collar of my large woolen overcoat.

"Just as soon as you want." He beamed, then pulled me into an embrace that almost crushed my ribs. "Keep working on that prototype," he whispered. "One day you will create a legend; of that I'm sure."

I tried to return his smile, but any idea of designing my revolutionary car seemed like a childish fantasy now.

As I clambered into the sidecar, Bertrand stretched out a hand stiffly to my father.

"Drive carefully," he told him.

Papa nodded solemnly, then pulled his goggles down and mounted the bike. He revved the engine several times and it spluttered, shocked by the cold, damp air. Finally we juddered out the gate and I watched the figure of Bertrand, tall and willowy as a reed, disappear from view.

As we plunged down the stony track and crested the hill on the other side, all was still. I was sure this was why my father had insisted on leaving so early—so he didn't have to suffer the indignity of passing Victor.

We entered the square, passing the closed shutters of the bar before beginning our descent out of the village. Immediately to our left was the little workshop where Camille's father had his forge. The door was open, but though I peered hard into the gloom, I couldn't make out any life inside.

I turned and faced forward, my heart sinking as I watched the village slip away behind me. An image suddenly popped into my head of Philippe smirking as he discovered how I'd skulked out of the village so early. The thought of him gloating left a taste like ash in my mouth.

Soon it was joined by something else: mud. Great mouthfuls of it were being thrown up as we bounced over every rut and pothole along the way.

I turned away to avoid the worst of it, and as I did so, I

suddenly spotted a figure standing way behind us, propped against the doorway to the forge. Even at this distance I recognized her immediately.

Camille.

Was it just chance, or had she come to see us off?

A few seconds later we turned the last corner on our way out of the village, and she was gone. But that fleeting glimpse of her had been enough to put the ghost of a smile back on my face.

Up ahead was a crossroads. To the left, a battered sign was tilted over, optimistically pointing toward Paris. My father waited as a horse and cart rattled past with several coffins loaded haphazardly on the back. I was wondering if they were occupied, when I suddenly realized that we weren't moving, even though the horse and cart had long since passed. I turned to look at Papa, and he pulled down his goggles and ran a large handkerchief over his face to wipe off the worst of the mud.

"What's wrong?" I asked.

He looked at me for what seemed an eternity before sighing heavily. "You realize that if we don't go back to Paris, your mother will never speak to me again?"

I held his look without blinking. "She doesn't speak to you anyway."

My father narrowed his eyes, then tugged off his gloves and threw them to me.

"What are these for?" I asked, hardly daring to hope.

"I assume you're driving," he announced with a gleam of mischief in his eye.

Was I hearing this right? My father was letting me drive

his treasured motorbike back into the village? I must have sat gaping at him, because after a moment he began to tug his gloves back on.

"Of course, if you don't want to go back . . ."

I didn't need asking twice. I sprang out of the sidecar and clambered onto the bike in front of my father. As I kicked the gear up to first and eased out the clutch, I revved a little too hard, and for a moment the sidecar lifted clean off the ground.

"Careful!" my father yelled over the racket from the engine. "You're going to kill us!"

But I had already turned the bike round and was accelerating back toward the village, leaving the lopsided sign still pointing to Paris.

13 My Mother's Reaction

"What do you mean you're not coming back to Paris!"

I could hear Maman's shocked voice from the other side of the hallway. Within minutes of arriving back at the house, my father had gulped down a shot of brandy, then rung my mother to break the news. I was perched on the stairs to listen, and judging by what I was hearing, she wasn't taking it well.

"Angelo has come up with an idea for a new car," my father reasoned. "Bertrand thinks it's worth exploring." My mother's response was so furious, he had to hold the receiver at arm's length. Some of what she said was too crackly, but the gist was easy enough to follow: over her dead body.

"Julietta, just listen to me," my father protested. "We're

only talking another week. Two at the most. We'll be back by Christmas—"

Suddenly he fell silent. My mother's voice had dropped so low I could no longer hear it. But I could see the impact of her words written across Papa's face.

"You don't think you're overreacting?" he muttered. I never heard the answer, and nor did he, because he suddenly glanced at the mouthpiece, then returned the phone to its cradle. She'd hung up.

By now I had been joined by Bertrand.

"I take it that didn't go as well as you hoped?" he asked with his usual flair for understatement.

"She says she's going to visit her father in Italy for a week. If Angelo's not home by the time she comes back," Papa said, eyeing me ominously, "she's coming to get you herself."

"Perfect!" Bertrand announced, clapping his hand against my back heartily. "Seven days should be more than enough."

I wanted to share his enthusiasm, but the gray look on my father's face worried me.

"Is that all she said?" I asked him cautiously.

He forced a smile. "She says you're to call her later. I think she needs some time to get used to the idea."

I could tell that he was holding something back, but I didn't know what. Whatever it was, I'd have to wait to find out, because Bertrand had already tugged on his trilby and thrown me my coat.

"Where are we going?" I asked, confused.

Ten minutes later we were standing in the middle of the test track again.

"Here?" my father asked, looking around in dismay.

"Where better to test-drive it?" Bertrand cried.

It was true. If we were going to design a car that could withstand any of the bumps and potholes rural France could throw at it, this was the spot.

My father groaned, clearly wondering how his once glorious career had been reduced to this, but Bertrand patted him on the back to console him.

"Don't worry. You're about to create a masterpiece. And to make sure of it, I've asked Pascal to give you whatever you need. He'll coordinate the entire project."

Pascal was in charge of all the company's most experimental projects back in Paris.

"I'll be back at the end of the week to see how you're getting on."

"Back?" I asked, thrown. "You mean you're not staying?"

"Me?" Bertrand chuckled wryly. "My dear boy, you think I can fritter away my time inventing crazy prototypes that may never see the light of day?" My father almost choked, but Bertrand was undeterred. "Besides, Antoine Pinay, the minister of munitions, has asked to speak to me. That's why you haven't a moment to lose."

My expression darkened. "Why?" I asked.

"Because if there is a war," my father replied, "the government will need the factory to make tanks and trucks for the front line."

"Exactly," Bertrand confirmed. "Your little car is far too important to be mothballed. A war with Germany might drag on for years. By then the Germans could have beaten us to your design. If they do that, the war's as good as lost anyway." He put one of his long hands on my shoulder.

"Anyway, if you're not finished soon, we'll have your mother to answer to."

The blood drained from my face at the thought of her sweeping into the village and taking me back to that dreaded school.

Bertrand had obviously read my mind. "Design the car, create a legend and make France proud," he urged me. "And wipe that smile off Victor's ferrety face."

By the time we arrived back at the house, we had a visitor. Christian was lounging in an armchair, smoking one of his exotic cigarettes and sipping a glass of champagne.

"I got Bertrand's telegram about some car that's going to make our careers and hopped on the first train down." He beamed. "I decided it called for a celebration."

Before my father could object, Christian had shoved a glass into my hand and was making a toast. "To history—and to peasants!"

14 Cyclops

"Even if we can get it to work, won't it be too heavy?" I asked tentatively.

It was the following morning, and we were standing gazing at the engine of the old ambulance.

Christian allowed the bonnet to slam shut and a panel snapped off where its hinges had rusted away.

"Tell me," he inquired, choking in the plume of dust that filled the air. "Is there any part of this project that isn't going to be difficult?"

I grinned unhelpfully. "That's why it's never been done before."

"Fine," he said. "Then perhaps you can tell us how to find an engine small enough to drive ten kilometers on one liter." This was the all-but-impossible test Bertrand had insisted on before he left. Only when this was achieved, he claimed, could the likes of Benoît and Marguerite afford to run the car.

I looked around as I racked my brain for possibilities. Suddenly my eyes alighted on something.

"Of course," I said brightly.

"Of course what?" my father snapped.

"Your motorbike."

He nearly choked. "Don't be absurd."

He looked from me to Christian and then back to me again.

"No. Absolutely not," he reiterated. "It's completely out of the question."

Less than an hour later, the motorbike lay in pieces across the gravel, looking more like the disemboweled carcass of an animal than a BMW Boxer. My father stood nearby, seething.

"I want every piece of this put back exactly as it was."

"Half of it was in the wrong place to start with," I said, looking up from where I was dismantling a section of exhaust.

Papa narrowed his eyes scornfully before stalking away. I could tell he was already regretting turning round at the crossroads.

As the days passed in a blur of activity, my father and Christian threw themselves passionately into designing the car. A couple of technicians from the Paris factory had been sent down to help build a corrugated-iron workshop in the field next to the test track. It was in here that the second prototype for the new car was starting to take shape, safely hidden from any prying eyes in the village. Several large padlocks secured the doors at night, just to be on the safe side.

Secrecy, Bertrand had insisted, was of the utmost importance. Rival companies were always trying to steal each other's designs to get one step ahead. One idle lapse in security, one blueprint carelessly left lying around, could spell the end of a project that had been years in the making.

There could be no slipups, Bertrand decreed. No one outside our immediate circle could know about our experimental new design. After all, who knew where our German rivals might have their spies? If our new design was going to be truly groundbreaking, we couldn't afford Porsche's people getting their hands on it. It wasn't just a matter of Bertrand's pride; somehow it was France's pride that was at stake now.

During this time I would sit for hours watching my father and Christian work and rework their sketches for the new prototype. It wasn't easy: the weather had turned bitterly cold again, and the little tin workshop felt like an icebox, especially when gusts of wind blew flurries of snow through the gaps in the walls. But I didn't care that my lips were turning blue and chapped, or that my fingers felt like they would snap off. All that mattered was that I was watching my father come alive again, totally absorbed in his work as he grappled with the all-but-impossible task.

At regular intervals, as the prototype slowly took shape, I would be called upon to cycle down the hill and up the other side to the forge to collect supplies. Félix had an old lock-up at the back of his workshop where he stored bits of machinery he'd rescued from every tractor or motorbike that had been abandoned in the village. There were even parts of an early German fighter plane that had been shot down during the Great War, including a small section of fuselage where the bullet holes could still be seen.

I kept hoping I would run into Camille when I called by the forge, just to see how her ankle was healing and to say sorry properly. But somehow she was always out on an errand or at school. Félix tried to assure me that it wasn't personal; that she was running errands for Marguerite, buying provisions for Christmas, which was now rapidly approaching. But I knew she was still angry with me.

Every evening I would wait patiently in the freezing hallway of the manor house for Maman to call from my grandparents' house in Italy. If the line worked, she would ring just before dinner, eager to talk to me—but never, I noticed, to my father. She would listen hungrily as I prattled on about how the prototype was coming along. I knew that, secretly, she thought we were wasting our time on yet another pipe dream, yet she always managed to sound excited for me.

I could tell she hated us being apart. I missed her too, much more than I'd expected. But deep down, I was also dreading her return. Going back to Paris and to Crespin's hateful dungeon felt like a fate worse than death.

So it was with mixed feelings that I waited for the following Sunday to come round. This was when my mother was due to return from Italy and I was to be put on a train to Paris.

The day before, Bertrand was due back from Paris to see

the inaugural test-drive of the new prototype. When he arrived at the track, my heart was thumping clean out of my chest. My father and Christian looked even more nervous.

They had every reason to be—they'd barely managed to bolt the prototype together, let alone test it.

Also present were the obligatory two chickens, which had been entrusted to my father's care. His face showed exactly how he felt about this honor, but it turned a deep puce when one of the birds, by now beside itself with nerves, produced a runny stream that dribbled down his jacket.

The stage was now set for the car's maiden voyage, but someone was still missing: Camille. She and her father were the only two villagers trusted enough to be invited to the test run—especially after we'd plundered Félix's secret treasure trove of engine parts. But where were they? Surely Camille couldn't still be furious with me?

Finally, just as I was ready to give up hope, I saw them trudging across the snow to join us, Félix carrying a large stone pitcher of wine under his arm. My heart surged, but before I could say anything, Christian was suddenly thrusting glasses of champagne into everyone's hands to celebrate the launch of our new prototype.

To be honest, it wasn't much to behold. In fact, it looked a lot like a cross between an old ambulance, a motorbike and a miniature pickup truck—which was exactly what it was.

The main body was welded together from several sheets of corrugated iron—the only metal light and flexible (not to mention available) enough. The windows were made of a glass substitute called mica, brought down from Paris, which was cheaper and lighter than glass. To keep costs down, there was also no mechanism for winding the windows down. Instead the driver could open a small hatch for ventilation or hand signals.

To further lighten the load, there was no roof. Instead, a canvas sheet had been stapled over the top to provide what I described grandly as a sun roof. Bertrand had scowled at this, thinking that it sounded like a luxury, but had eventually been persuaded.

The final touch was the headlamp. Not two like in normal cars, but one large one perched proudly in the middle of the bonnet. This had been my father's "master stroke," as he saw it.

"It looks like a cyclops," Christian had quipped, earning a dirty look from my father.

Only one feature had survived from my earlier lawn mower prototype: the canvas seats. It was agreed that these were a clever addition as they were light and would help soften what was bound to be a bumpy ride. Two additional hammock-style seats had duly been salvaged from the old German biplane parts in Félix's secret lock-up.

The big question now was: would the car pass the all-important test of crossing a plowed field with two chickens, a flagon of wine and a dozen eggs?

I leaped forward and gave the starter handle a vigorous yank. With a splutter of black smoke, the car exploded into life, almost rattling the corrugated iron clean off its rivets. The starter handle promptly shook itself loose and landed on the ground. Undaunted, everyone broke into spontaneous applause.

"I think you should be the first to try it," Christian told Bertrand.

"It would be a privilege," he said, glowing. "But I will require a copilot." He gave me a sidelong glance and I beamed back eagerly.

The inside of the cab was so tiny that Bertrand almost had to double himself up to squeeze in behind the wheel; his trilby was knocked off as he crouched under the "sun roof."

"Hold on," I said. I grabbed one of the corners of the canvas top and gave it a sharp tug. With a loud *pop!* it came away from the fasteners holding it onto the frame, and I rolled it back till Bertrand was able to stretch his bald head out through the roof. I then handed him back his trilby and he put it on again; it peeped out above the top of the car by a full ten centimeters.

"Wait!" My father rushed forward. "Don't forget the rest of your passengers." And he squeezed the indignant chickens through the tiny window. One of the birds settled on my lap, but the other immediately flapped itself into a frenzy, sending Bertrand's trilby flying again, before clambering out through the sun roof. Here it took up position in a sort of makeshift crow's nest.

Christian handed me his tray of eggs. "Look after them carefully," he urged me solemnly.

I nodded and cradled them on my lap while trying to hold on to the other chicken, which wanted to be up on the roof too. Félix carefully placed the flagon of wine on the backseat.

"Ready?" Bertrand called out to me over the racket of the

engine. I nodded uncertainly, and he eased his foot off the clutch.

The car jolted into life, immediately tipping an egg over the edge of the tray. I managed to grab it before it broke, but lost my grip on the outraged chicken. It immediately flapped up onto the roof and perched beside the other one.

Bertrand concentrated hard on edging the car forward, and it gradually began to build up momentum.

At first all seemed well. But then, as the car gathered a fraction more speed, it began to groan ominously, just as the lawn mower had. Soon the corrugated iron was bending and distorting under the strain of holding itself together. The suspension was doing its job, but the superstructure was now locked into a sickening cyclical gyration, as though the car was swinging its hips from side to side in a demented rumba.

I looked around, unnerved. "Is it supposed to do that?"

Bertrand gripped the wheel till his knuckles went white. "Forget that. Are the eggs broken?"

"Not yet," I shouted back.

"Then it can do whatever it wants."

He pressed the tiny accelerator pedal to the floor, and the car leaped forward with a loud backfire. The two chickens immediately abandoned ship, wisely deciding to cut their losses early.

Bertrand tugged the steering wheel to the left, and we veered off the track toward the plowed field beyond. Suddenly I had an alarming flashback to my crash with the lawn mower, which had nearly broken Camille's ankle.

"Are you sure this is a good idea?" I asked, trying to keep the rising panic out of my voice.

"We have to see what she's made of, don't we?" he boomed back, urging the little car toward the field.

"But what if we crash again?" I called out.

"Have a little faith!" Bertrand insisted.

Suddenly the car hit the first rut, and I braced myself for instant self-destruction. But to my surprise, it held together far better than I'd feared. Only two eggs jumped out of the tray and broke, covering my boots with their creamy orange yolks.

But if the front suspension coped better than expected, the rear was a different matter. The moment it hit the rut, the car grounded itself, the axle grinding against the wheel arch with a horrible crunch.

Bertrand immediately winced as pain shot up his back. "I think I just fused two of my vertebrae," he groaned.

But I had become distracted by something else. A smell of burning had enveloped the car. I glanced down at my feet to see silver sparks flashing from the floor. Suddenly there was a fizz and a crack like a sodium lightbulb, and the foot-well sizzled into flames.

"We're on fire!" I cried.

Bertrand glanced over to see more sparks flying up from the metal chassis. "Blast!" he cursed, before slamming the brakes on. "And we were doing so well."

As quickly as we could, we bundled out of what was left of the car: just in time, as it turned out. The sparks ignited the canvas hammock seats, and they went up in a burst of multicolored flame.

"Something tells me we didn't pass the test," I sighed as the others raced over the field toward us.

But Bertrand was more philosophical. "A few minor adjustments. Nothing more."

Suddenly the tires popped with a loud hiss, and the car slumped down onto its rear end as if someone had pulled a chair out from under it.

15 Back to the Drawing Board

"A short circuit in the electrics caused a spark to ignite the magnesium in the suspension arm," Christian announced blithely. "It can be solved easily."

I wasn't entirely sure what any of this meant, but apparently the car's maiden voyage hadn't been a complete disaster after all, despite combusting and leaving a large scorched patch in the middle of the test track. Christian had insisted on bringing us all to Victor's bar to toast its success. I think the real reason was to try and cheer me up. Everyone knew that today was my last day. Tomorrow I would be taking the train home to my mother—and my hated school.

I say Christian had invited everyone, but Camille hadn't joined us. As soon as she'd reassured herself Bertrand was unharmed after the car blew up, she made an excuse about having another errand to run and slipped away. As I watched her trudge across the field, I was convinced the real reason she was leaving was because she was disgusted with me for causing yet another crash.

Moments later I noticed something glinting in the long grass. Reaching down, I discovered it was a small brooch. I'd seen Camille wearing something identical once before. It was nothing elaborate—rather scuffed and worn, in fact, in the crude shape of a beetle.

I thought about rushing after her to give it back, but before I could, Christian had wrapped an arm around me and insisted we head straight to the bar.

With his usual flourish, Christian was now demanding another bottle of the finest champagne, but since he'd already exhausted the bar's entire supply, Victor was heading over with a bottle of Benoît's homemade concoction. As I stared at the dusty bottle, I couldn't help thinking that it looked like murky pond water. I swore I even saw a tadpole swimming around in it.

"A lot of the locals are talking about you setting off some fireworks." Victor grinned, clearly enjoying poking fun at our car. "Are we celebrating?"

Bertrand carefully folded the blueprints to prevent him from seeing anything too revealing. He smiled, giving away as little as possible. "Just some initial experiments . . . ," he said.

"Surely you're not still trying to make that car of yours?" Victor asked me, with a hint of a sneer. "I thought after what happened to Camille you might have seen sense."

I could feel my jaw tightening with dislike for him, but Papa got in first.

"If you're so sure it can't be done, perhaps you'd like to put a small wager on it," he said, icy cool.

Victor raised a playful eyebrow. This was fighting talk indeed. "How about dinner for everyone here. The winner pays."

"Done," my father replied, stretching a hand out to shake.

"May the best man win—or should I say boy." Victor grinned, showing his yellow teeth. With that, he wandered back to join his cronies at the bar.

My father scowled as he watched him. "Arrogant monkey!"

"Relax," Bertrand soothed. "Victor is not our enemy."

"Then who is?" I asked, recoiling from the rancid smell of Benoît's potion.

"Germany, for a start," my father grumbled into his glass.

"We have a more immediate problem than that," Bertrand insisted. "The suspension. Until we find a way to even out those bumps, we're never going to win that bet of yours."

Christian spread the blueprints across the table again. "What we need is a suspension system where the back wheels know what the front wheels are doing."

"You mean you want the front wheels to talk to the back wheels?" I asked doubtfully.

"Exactly," Christian replied without batting an eyelid. "Somehow we need the front wheels to warn the back wheels that a bump is coming so the car doesn't bounce so high . . ."

"And how precisely will you achieve all this?" Papa asked doubtfully.

Christian shrugged. "I haven't the foggiest—but that never stopped us before."

"How long will all this take?" Bertrand asked, a little impatient now.

"Six months, maybe a year."

"A year?" my father cried, clearly horrified at the idea of being trapped in this village so long.

"Too long," Bertrand barked. "I want this finished and in production before the Germans try to steal it."

"But why would they be interested in a rusty old heap of junk that blows up?" I scoffed.

Bertrand turned and looked at me so fiercely that I shrank back into my seat.

"I told you. Ferdinand Porsche is already developing his own people's car. As soon as he finds out we're trying to beat him to it, he'll try to sabotage us—or steal our design. Believe me," he went on somberly, "if we go to war and the Germans invade, the first people to cross the border will be storm troopers. The second will be his car engineers."

I gasped. "You think he knows about it already?"

"I'm certain of it."

"It's not just Porsche you have to worry about," my father added. "If this suspension is going to be as clever as we hope, the Nazis will want to steal it for the military."

I felt a chill run down my spine. I glanced over my shoulder and looked at Victor, gossiping with his friends. If Porsche really did have his spies everywhere, as Bertrand suspected, was it possible that our greatest enemy was already among us?

Either way, there wasn't much I could do about it now. Tomorrow I would be leaving the village, probably forever. Whatever changes were made to the prototype, they would have to be made without me.

The thought of heading back weighed heavily on me as I trudged out into the cold night air. I sulkily kicked a stone around the square until my father slipped out of the bar to join me.

"Will you at least come back to Paris for Christmas?" I asked gloomily.

"Of course," he reassured me. "Now let's get back to the house before we die of cold."

He turned to head across the square, but there was something I knew I needed to do before I left.

"I'm going to call by the smithy. I want to try out some ideas for the suspension," I announced, not altogether convincingly.

"Don't be too late," my father said.

A few moments later I approached the forge and took a deep breath. Reaching into my pocket, I felt the pin of Camille's brooch prick my fingertip. I mustered all my courage and rapped lightly on the door. Félix glanced up, surprised to see me.

"I wondered if I could speak to Camille," I asked cautiously. "I think I found something of hers."

"She's upstairs. But mind you don't keep her too long," he said gruffly. "She's doing her schoolwork."

I made my way up the stairs to their apartment and knocked on the door tentatively. Getting no answer, I gently pushed it open.

"Hello?"

The room was empty. I was beginning to think that maybe this wasn't such a good idea after all when my eyes alighted on a small attic window. Peering through it, I spotted a hunched figure sitting on the roof.

"Camille?"

She spun round. "What do you want?" she said with a scowl.

"I—I found something of yours," I stammered. "After the test run."

"After the fireworks display, you mean?"

I felt the hairs on the back of my neck bristle at her put-down. "Fine, if you don't want it . . ." I turned to head back down, but she quickly stopped me.

"I was only teasing. Show me—please."

I clambered up through the window and stepped out onto the roof. As I did so, I caught a glimpse of the cobbled street three floors below and my head began to swim sickeningly.

Camille was watching me closely. "Does it scare you?" she asked. The idea seemed to amuse her.

"No," I lied. "What are you doing up here anyway?"

"It's the only place I can be alone," she answered, before adding: "Usually."

I ignored her little dig and edged across the roof toward her. She wriggled over a few inches to make room, and I squeezed down beside her. Digging into my pocket for the brooch, I held it out to her.

"My scarab beetle!" she cried. Her fingers felt warm on my palm as she took it gratefully. "Where did you find it?"

"You must have dropped it after the test run. What is a scarab beetle, anyway?"

"A dung beetle. The ancient Egyptians wore them as good luck charms," she replied, pinning it back onto her cardigan. "Apparently the way they rolled up little balls of dung reminded them of the heavenly cycles. Don't ask me why."

"So you wear it to bring you luck?"

"No," she answered matter-of-factly. "I wear it because my mother gave it to me."

I glanced at her, curious. It was the first time I'd heard her mention her mother. "So where is she now?" As soon as the words were out of my mouth I wished I could take them back. "Sorry, I didn't mean to stick my nose in."

"It's okay." She shrugged. "She died when I was little. That's why I didn't want to lose it."

I nodded, and for a minute neither of us spoke.

"So," Camille said. "What's the real reason you came up here? And don't say to return my brooch. You could have handed that to anyone to give back to me."

For a second I was taken aback by her directness. Then I decided I would be just as direct back.

"I wanted to say goodbye."

"Goodbye?" If she was faking her shock, she was doing a good job of it, because for a split second she sounded almost disappointed.

"I have to go home to Paris tomorrow."

Camille frowned. "You sound like you don't want to. I thought you'd be jumping for joy."

"Going back's the last thing I want."

Again, she looked genuinely surprised. "You can't honestly want to stay here?"

"I want to see our car design through to the end."

"Oh, that," she groaned. "At this rate you're going to run out of people to break."

"Look, I'm sorry about your ankle," I said, managing not to sound the least bit sorry. "But if we can make this work, it will be . . . well . . ." I caught a glimpse of her looking at me skeptically and lost my nerve. "What's the point? You wouldn't understand."

"I understand you're obsessed with that thing. It's like you're trying to prove something. How much better you are because you come from the big city, no doubt."

I couldn't believe what I was hearing. "Is that what everyone thinks? That I'm just trying to show off?"

"Aren't you?"

I stared at her for a moment, then turned and looked out across the rooftops, my blood boiling.

"Sorry," she said sheepishly. "That came out worse than it was meant to."

But I wasn't ready to forgive her so easily. Seeing that I was still sulking, she got to her feet.

"I should go. My father will be wondering where I am—"

"Wait," I said. I couldn't let her leave without explaining. "The reason I'm obsessed with the car is because I destroyed my dad's last one. Flattened, to be precise. It could cost him his job."

Camille took this in for a moment. "So now you're trying to build another one to make it up to him?"

"Except that I destroyed that as well," I said despondently.

She studied me closely, all signs of her earlier spikiness gone. For the first time since I'd arrived in the village, I thought she almost looked sympathetic. But before she could say anything, her father called up from downstairs.

"I have to go," Camille said, turning to head back through the window. Before she went, she paused and smiled. "I hope you get to build your car one day. Goodbye, Angelo."

And with that she was gone.

After she'd left, I sat by myself for a while, staring out across the rooftops into the great black unknown. After my excitement at turning back at the crossroads and roaring into the village on my father's motorbike, I couldn't believe all my hopes had come to nothing.

Eventually I climbed down, somehow managing not to dash my brains out on the cobbles below, and set out across the square for home. After a couple of meters, however, a crunch of gravel alerted me to someone behind.

"Hello?" I said, peering suspiciously into the darkness.

Silence greeted my question. I was about to head away when I heard it again. Someone was definitely out there— and now they were approaching. A prickle of fear tugged at my collar.

"Who's out there?"

A figure suddenly loomed out of the darkness.

Philippe.

"Oh, it's you," I said, trying not to betray any fear.

He was staring at me coldly. "I wonder what her father would say if he knew you'd been meeting his daughter up here."

"Actually, he sent me up there," I replied, trying to sound confident but not succeeding. "Not that it's any of your business."

Philippe took a few steps closer, his eyes icy with hatred. "You know, he isn't really her father."

"What?" I mumbled, confused.

"Her mother was a German sympathizer during the war. And Camille's real father was German."

For a second I was too dumbstruck to form any kind of response.

"I guess that makes her the enemy in this war," he sneered, before looking me up and down. "Angelo. Italian, isn't it?"

"What if it is?" I answered, my mouth dry.

Philippe leaned in close, his breath filling the air with steam. "They say your lot are going to join the Germans. So I guess you and Camille will both be on the enemy's side." He suddenly spat in my face. "Traitor!"

I felt a fog of rage envelop me, and I was about to leap at him when a voice called out from the road just beyond.

"Angelo?"

I spun round to see my father approaching.

"Did I interrupt anything?" he asked suspiciously.

For a moment I was paralyzed. Should I tell him about Philippe's vile accusations?

"Philippe was just telling me how fascinated he is by foreign cultures," I heard myself say sarcastically. I didn't want to be beaten up by Philippe, but equally I wasn't having my father fighting my battles for me.

Philippe glanced at me suspiciously, clearly wondering if

this was some kind of game. In the end he obviously decided I wasn't worth the bother, and sloped off into the night.

"What were you fighting about?" my father asked.

I thought about lying, then decided against it.

"Camille."

"Ah. You've made an enemy there, then," Papa observed.

"I don't know why. She clearly hates me as much as he does. Anyway, what does it matter, if I'm leaving in the morning?"

"Actually, that's what I came to tell you. You may not be able to."

I felt my heart about to burst with relief—but why wasn't my father more excited about this miraculous change of events? "Your mother rang to say she's stuck in Italy," he continued, more solemn now. "She can't travel back tomorrow after all."

"Why?" I asked, suddenly feeling a twinge of anxiety.

"Italy has sided with Germany," my father explained. "If there's a war, they'll be the enemy. France isn't letting anyone else in or out across the border."

If I'd been ecstatic about the news that I didn't need to go home tomorrow, now I felt only panic.

"Will she be okay?"

"Absolutely. It just means that for the moment she has to stay put with her father. And you will have to stay here. You can imagine she's pretty upset about it."

By now my mind was crowded with thoughts. My father must have seen my alarm, because he put a comforting hand on my shoulder.

"Everything will be fine, I promise. For now, we must keep ourselves busy with that confounded car of yours. Finishing that is more important than ever now."

But another, darker fear had crept into my thoughts.

"What about you?" I asked grimly.

"What about me?"

"You're Italian. Won't you be seen as the enemy too? They might think you're some kind of spy. . . ."

My imagination was in danger of running away with me. Was Philippe right after all? Would my father end up an enemy in his own country?

But Papa ran an affectionate thumb over my cheek.

"If I manage to make this car, they won't think I'm the enemy. I'll be a national hero. And it'll all be down to you."

He swept me up into his arms and held me tightly for the first time since I'd destroyed his car at the motor show.

16 The Beauty Contest

Christmas in the village of Regnac should have been idyllic.
The morning broke with a gentle flutter of snowflakes that
left a light dusting like caster sugar over the frozen fields and
streams. Everything was sparkling. But despite my relief at
being able to stay and help with work on the next prototype,
I was worried about my mother.

Coming to the village was supposed to help bring my parents closer together—or so I'd foolishly hoped. Now they
were farther apart than ever. And with talk of war becoming
more urgent all the time, the likelihood of Maman returning anytime soon was receding.

At least I had the car to distract me. Work on the next
model began almost before Marguerite's Christmas pudding
had been eaten. With our bellies still stuffed with rabbit

and foie gras from Benoît's farmyard, Christian, my father and I slipped away from the table early and tramped across the snow-covered fields to start work inside the freezing tin workshop.

There, day after day, and sometimes straight through the night, we could be heard hammering and drilling and welding new designs—always behind locked doors to keep prying eyes at bay. No one outside our small circle was allowed to know what we were up to—especially not Victor or his son.

As for Philippe and his poisonous remarks about Camille's mother, I decided to ignore them. I'd be lying if I said I wasn't desperate to ask her about it, but that felt like it would be playing straight into Philippe's hands, so I kept my questions to myself.

Far more important was the problem of the car's suspension. But as days turned into weeks and then months, Christian's dream of getting the front wheels to "speak" to the back seemed nothing more than that: a dream. How long could it be before the Germans beat us to it and Bertrand's nightmare came true?

There was one small breakthrough, however: a problem with the water freezing in the car's cooler system was fixed—mainly because the weather finally stopped being so cold. The last of the snow showers passed and the ground slowly thawed, opening itself invitingly to the first warm rays of the sun. The muddy ruts, until recently full to the brim with freezing slush, dried and became soft and gooey like cake batter.

During this time my mother rang from Italy every day. Between us, me, my father and Christian had constructed an elaborate lie to fool her into thinking I was going to school. To be fair, my father did have some vague notion that something ought to be done, and even made some inquiries about me starting at the village school, along with Camille. But the threat of war made it seem rather pointless.

After a while, even Maman stopped nagging about it, and accepted—for the moment, at least—that I was better off hidden in the depths of the countryside, far away from any potential German invasion. Or Italian, for that matter.

Gradually my father, Christian and I become regulars in Victor's bar. Papa would rather have gone almost anywhere else, but since there wasn't anywhere else, he had no choice. There was also the small matter of Dominique—or rather, her confectioneries.

Whether it was her croissants stuffed with praline fondant or her chocolate-centered macaroons, we were hooked. I think that was why my father seemed to relax about being imprisoned, as he called it, in the village. So long as he had a supply of sticky delicacies and strong, sweet coffee, he wasn't grumbling—or not much more than normal, anyway.

My memory of the little café and pâtisserie across the road from the workshop in Paris, where our adventure had first started, slowly faded as I melted into village life.

A second plate of macaroons was now sitting empty on our table, along with several glasses of frothing lager and a soda for me.

Christian, unsurprisingly, was an incorrigible gambler, and I had now been instructed in the dark art of poker—Texas Hold 'em, to be precise.

To begin with, we used empty pistachio shells as betting

chips. But as the weeks and months passed, the pistachio shells were replaced with small change and then small-denomination notes.

More often than not, Benoît joined us. He would sit sipping his pastis noisily, his two teeth rattling on the rim of the glass. At regular intervals, his daughter, Amandine, would bustle into the bar to bark an order at him to come home for dinner. Short and thickset, and barely out of her teens, she already had a large mole like her mother's jutting out of her chin. Benoît would nod and reassure her that he was about to come, then pour himself another pastis and stay exactly where he was.

Félix was also a regular player. But as he said virtually nothing beyond the odd grunt and his face never gave anything away, it was impossible to work out if he had a good hand or not.

Dominique would generally hover somewhere near the back, preferring the anonymity of the shadows. I had learned from Benoît that, as well as making chocolate, Dominique had once been a promising musician. She might even have been a star, but when she met Victor in her teens, she had fallen completely under his spell. Now—except for special occasions—she almost never played, preferring to keep her viola carefully packed away.

Seeing that our plate was empty, she was now heading over to replace it. As she slid a fresh saucer of pistachio macaroons onto the table, Christian looked up and caught her eye. His smile was so dazzling and infectious, it seemed to startle her. She lost her grip and the saucer fell to the floor, cracking in two. As we quickly scrambled to pick up the biscuits, Christian kept reassuring her that no harm had been done.

"See," he said, dusting one of them off and popping it whole into his mouth. "As delicious as ever."

Flustered, Dominique smiled shyly and hurried back into the kitchen.

"Funny, isn't it," Christian sighed after a moment, watching her disappear. "Beautiful women in villages like this. They always end up married to potbellied oafs like Victor."

Benoît chuckled, his chest rattling. "You know, she turned me down once," he rasped. "Probably because I only have a farm while Victor has a bar."

"Or because you're old enough to be her grandfather, you old scoundrel," Christian snorted.

"I thought you were already married?" I asked Benoît.

"Marguerite's only my first wife," he joked with a roguish smile, before placing another bet. "If you really want to chat Dominique up, you'll be wanting to come to the beauty contest tomorrow."

"Victor's wife's in a beauty contest?" Christian asked, even more intrigued.

"Not his wife, you fool. Cows."

"You're having a beauty contest for cows?" I asked, bewildered.

"And pigs. We hold it every year in my barn. Come along, if you like."

"I can't think of anything I'd rather do," my father said insincerely as he played what he clearly assumed was his winning hand. "Three jacks." He started to scoop up his winnings, only for me to show my four tens, trumping him easily.

Papa narrowed his eyes at me sardonically. "Tomorrow you definitely start school."

The following evening we strolled down the hill from the test track to Benoît's barn, where a large party was already in full swing. As we entered, it was hard to tell which smelled more rank—the cow dung or the unique aroma of Benoît's home brew.

Benoît himself was sitting at one end of the barn playing a long snakelike instrument called a serpent. A distant relative of the tuba, it was made of walnut, with six finger holes like a recorder. Benoît's cheeks were puffed out like a gnarly old toad's as he blew on the strange twisted horn.

At his side sat Victor, his large beer belly heaving in and out as he squeezed his accordion. He was accompanied by several other locals on a collection of instruments, including Félix on a huge French horn.

Tucked away to one side sat Dominique, playing her viola. The annual beauty contest, it turned out, was one of the few occasions when she still got to play, and she threw herself wholeheartedly into the folk tunes and ballads.

Marguerite was in charge of pouring out beer and wine from several stone flagons set up on a long trestle table at the back. Amandine was also helping. I saw her cheeks flush radioactively as Christian asked her for three tankards. She handed them over, batting her eyelids, until she saw her mother glowering at her.

Christian brought the beer back over and Papa eyed his tankard with suspicion.

"Are you sure this isn't for external use only?"

"The trick is not to smell it," Christian assured him.

My father held his nose and poured the entire tankard down his throat in one go. As he finished the last drop, he wiped his chin and took a moment to reflect.

"I can definitely say that it tastes every bit as bad as it smells." He handed his tankard to Christian. "Fill me up."

Meanwhile, I glanced around the barn and spotted Camille whispering into the ear of one of Benoît's prize cows. She was wearing a checked frock specially for the occasion, and her hair was hanging loose, a tangle of unruly red curls almost covering the tiny dung beetle I saw pinned to her cardigan.

Suddenly I realized that I was being watched. Philippe was glaring malevolently at me from the other side of the barn. Since the night we'd nearly come to blows, I had hardly seen him. In fact, I'd even begun to wonder if he was steering clear of me, embarrassed by his vicious outburst. But if he was, he wasn't looking guilty now; he looked like he wanted to kill me.

I wasn't going to be intimidated, though. Undaunted, I walked across to Camille, feeling the heat of Philippe's gaze with every step.

"You're late," she said, looking up at me with a wry smile. "We've already judged the pig contest."

"I only came to wish you luck," I said with a smirk. As I sat down beside her, I noticed that for once she didn't move away.

"You know Philippe is still staring at you," she said after a moment.

Before I could answer, my nostrils caught a scent of something sweet and exotic.

"Do you smell that?" I asked, my nose twitching inquisitively.

"Émilie's been at the artichokes again," she replied, nodding to Benoît's cow, which was munching away contentedly.

"No . . . it's chocolate." My eyes scoped the barn. Sure enough, there on a table near the back was a vat of Dominique's legendary dark hot chocolate.

Moments later I was bent over my mug, allowing the steam to waft around my face like a soft chocolaty blanket— just like I used to in the café back in Paris.

"You always do that, don't you?" Camille said, watching me curiously.

"What?"

"Stick your face in it and grin like an idiot."

"No, I don't." But of course I did.

"I'm going outside," I said abruptly, and began to head out into the darkness.

After a moment Camille joined me on the damp grass outside. The air was crisp and cool after the sweaty beer fumes in the barn.

"So, have you finished that car yet?" she inquired. "Everyone's talking about your bet with Victor."

"Yeah, well, at this rate he's going to win," I muttered. "Anyway, I'm not allowed to talk about it."

"Why?" she asked casually. "Because I might be a German spy?"

For a moment I didn't know what to say. Did she know the vicious rumor Philippe was spreading about her? Before I could ask, a shadow fell across us.

Philippe had left the barn and was now studying me coldly. I felt my fingers clench instinctively into a fist. If he was going to attack me, I would make sure I left him with at least something to show for it.

"Having a cozy little chat?" he sneered. "I should have known you two would be whispering together."

"Why?" Camille asked. "Are you jealous?"

"Of a kid like him?" He turned and looked at me with undiluted hatred. "If there's a war, I'm going to make sure I get posted to the border with Italy," he spat. "That way the first person I kill will be a dirty Italian, just like you!"

It was all I could do not to let fly at him there and then. But instead I swallowed my anger, pretending to be confused.

"That's strange. . . ." I frowned. "Last I heard, your daddy was going to make sure you worked in a back office somewhere so you never had to fire a shot—"

I was about to congratulate myself on my clever put-down when my head was filled with a blinding flash. Philippe's fist had crunched into my jaw like a train hitting the buffers. Next thing I knew, I could taste dirt in my mouth and was sprawled on the ground.

At first everything was blurred. I shook my head in a desperate attempt to get my eyes to refocus, until at last I was looking at just one of Philippe again, towering over me. Suddenly I heard a strangled growl welling up from somewhere deep inside me; then I launched myself at him with everything I had.

Philippe obviously wasn't expecting it: he was sent flying, thumping into the dirt with me still clinging to him like a demented attack dog.

For a moment the pair of us were locked together, writhing around in the dirt as Camille shrieked at us to stop. Finally she managed to prize my arms off Philippe and drag me away.

Suddenly free, Philippe sprang to his feet and was about to unleash another blow with one of his huge iron fists when Camille threw herself in front of him, eyes bulging wildly.

"You want to get to him, you go through me," she hissed venomously.

"This is nothing to do with you," Philippe seethed, his chest heaving.

"He's right." I gasped, the pain in my jaw making me want to throw up. "He thinks just because I'm Italian I'm going to side with Germany."

"Aren't you?" Philippe jeered.

"Of course not!" I protested. "France is my home now, the same as you."

"You and me will never be the same! So why don't you go back to where you came from. Traitor!"

Before I could take my revenge, Camille had stepped forward, inches from Philippe's face, her jaw hardening with hatred.

"And I suppose I'm a Nazi spy, am I, because my father was German?"

So it was true. Félix wasn't her real father.

Philippe fixed her with a cold, insolent stare. "You tell me. . . ."

Camille was about to slap him but, fast as lightning, Philippe grabbed her hand and held it menacingly before shoving it away. His eyes were burning with anger and jealousy, but there was something else there as well—a hint of shame. But if he was sorry for what he'd said, he wasn't about to admit it. Giving me a last disdainful look, he turned and stalked away into the night.

I took a deep breath, then coughed up another mouthful of dirt and blood as Camille held out her hand to me. I grabbed it and let her help me to my feet. For a moment I thought I was going to fall over again—my head was swirling sickeningly—but I managed to stay upright.

"We should put some of Benoît's home brew on that," she said, eyeing the cut that was starting to throb on my lip. "You know it's legendary for its healing powers." But the thought of putting Benoît's concoction anywhere near my mouth made my head reel again.

"Come on." She smiled at me. "We can still catch the results."

17 A Legend Is Born

"I won't be able to stay long," Bertrand hollered above the noise of the axles crunching over the ruts in the road. It was several weeks after the beauty contest, and I was sitting in his car, bumping along the dirt road to the test track. He had popped down from Paris to pay a surprise visit to the workshop as soon as he'd heard our news.

A few nights before, Christian had finally had the breakthrough he'd been searching for. He'd come crashing into the house, screaming so loudly I'd thought it was burning down. But when I scrambled downstairs, I found him dancing around the breakfast room with my father as though they had gotten into Benoît's homemade brew.

Lying on the table was a rusty old drainpipe.

"What is it?" I asked, still groggy from being so rudely awakened.

"It's the new suspension system, of course!" Christian cried. Seeing my confusion, he grabbed it and proceeded to demonstrate by shoving a poker up one end. Inside was some sort of shock absorber. As the poker squeezed, the spring inside it forced a lever out the other end of the pipe.

Christian and my father turned to me, grinning idiotically.

"Isn't it genius?" Christian exclaimed. "It's so simple I can't believe I didn't see it before."

"See what?" I asked, completely stumped.

"Imagine the front wheel is attached to the poker. When it hits the bump, the shock forces the poker into the drainpipe like this." He shoved the poker in. "Now, imagine the poker on the other end is connected to the back wheel. As the poker is forced out the back end, it pushes down on the suspension, tightening it so that it can't bounce so high. It's a miracle!" he cried.

Slowly a smile crept across my face as I realized the full impact of what he was saying. If he was right, the front wheel would effectively be able to warn the back wheel that a bump was coming. In other words, they would be able to talk to each other.

Suddenly there were not two but three people dancing around the breakfast room, shouting for joy.

"Why do you have to go back so soon?" I shouted across to Bertrand as we approached the test track.

"I have to be in Paris tonight. The board are meeting

to discuss what we'll do if war is declared. They want us to design a new six-wheeled gun tractor."

I felt a trickle of cold sweat down my back again. For months I'd felt cocooned from the real world, hidden away in the depths of the countryside. I'd been too busy working on the car to think much about the war. But now there was no escaping it. With Germany amassing a vast army of Porsche's Panzer tanks, threatening to overrun its smaller neighbors, it was all too horribly real.

Bertrand swung the car through the open gate and pulled up near the workshop. But before he climbed out, there was something I had been itching to ask him.

"Camille . . ." I hesitated. "You never mentioned that her father was a German deserter."

"Who told you that?" he asked sternly.

"Philippe."

Bertrand's face clouded. "I should have known. But for the record, he wasn't a deserter. His plane was shot down."

I gasped. "You mean, all those parts in Félix's lock-up . . . ?"

". . . were from his plane, yes. His name was Ulrich," he explained. "After he was shot down, he staggered to Hélène's house—that was Camille's mother. The local militia were out hunting him, but Hélène refused to give him up. She must have felt sorry for him, I suppose." He shot me a quizzical look from under his bushy eyebrows. "Do you think less of Camille now?"

"No," I answered honestly.

"Good," he said. "Because her father was a good man. He was just on the other side."

"What happened after that?" I asked.

"Hélène hid him in a secret cellar under the floorboards for months on end—till the war was over, in fact. During that time they must have gradually fallen in love."

"And after the war?"

"They moved away. Far enough away for no one to know Ulrich's true identity. For years I didn't hear anything—until one day, out of the blue, Hélène came home . . . with Camille. She must only have been a year or so old."

"Where was her father?"

"He'd died. Something to do with the mustard gas they'd used during the war, I think."

"And Félix?"

"Hélène married him a few years later. An old tractor he was working on had toppled over backward and would have killed Camille if Félix hadn't put himself in harm's way."

"Was that how he got his limp?" I asked, suddenly piecing everything together.

Bertrand nodded. "He was so strong and kind, Hélène couldn't help but love him for it." He smiled to himself as he recollected. "How he doted on that child. He couldn't have adored her more if she'd been his own. But then, a few years later, Hélène became ill and died as well. Some say she'd never really got over losing Ulrich."

He paused to stuff a little tobacco into his pipe, then lit it. "Now, enough gossip. We have work to do."

Perhaps there was more to this story, but for the moment I felt I'd intruded enough.

I followed him round to the front of the workshop, where we found Christian puffing on one of his exotic cigarettes. When he saw us, he almost swallowed it in shock.

"What are you doing here?" he spluttered.

"We've come to inspect the car," Bertrand announced brightly. "I assume it's ready."

"I'm afraid you've had a wasted journey," Christian told us abruptly. "It's not finished yet. You should have given us a few more days." But I could tell from his caginess that he was hiding something.

Bertrand obviously thought the same.

"Can't we at least look at it? After all, I've come all this way."

"I'm afraid that's out of the question. I'll call you as soon as there's news."

There was no doubting it—Christian was acting very oddly. What was it he was so desperate to hide?

Before Bertrand or I had a chance to ask, the sound of a car noisily starting up made us turn toward the workshop.

"Why are the doors closed?" Bertrand asked suspiciously.

"We've run into some problems with the water-cooled engine again," Christian blurted.

"What kind of problems?"

"The water froze."

"But it's nearly summer," Bertrand retorted.

For a moment Christian looked lost for words before finally sighing. "All we need is a few more days. We've had some teething problems . . . with the styling."

"The styling . . . ?" Bertrand echoed, looking confused. "What styling? This is supposed to be a functional machine for farmers."

But before Christian had a chance to explain, the doors

to the workshop flew open, and a car unlike anything I had seen before burst out and slewed to a halt in front of us.

At the wheel sat my father, grinning from behind a set of grimy goggles.

"Well? What do you think?" he asked proudly, leaping out.

Bertrand glanced at Christian, who was now looking un-characteristically sheepish.

"This is what you wouldn't show me?"

Christian shrugged, and without a word Bertrand went over to examine the car.

Like the earlier model, it was made from panels of corrugated iron. But instead of the flatbed trailer, the new prototype boasted four makeshift seats and a roof that swept down toward the back. On either side, two bright yellow wheel arches concealed the rear wheels so that only the bottom peeked out.

Bertrand slowly paced his way around the car, his expression giving little away. "Something about these yellow panels . . . ," he noted dryly. "They seem strangely familiar."

My father smiled. "I made a little trip down to the river."

I glanced back at the car and realized that he had stripped much of the bodywork from Christian's bright yellow sports car, still buried in the riverbed.

"I also see the countryside has influenced your design," Bertrand observed, arching an eyebrow.

"What makes you say that?" Papa frowned.

"Simple," Bertrand announced. "From the front it looks like a toad and from the back like a constipated duck."

"I think it looks more like a snail," I ventured, then quickly realized my mistake when my father glared at me.

"A tin snail, perhaps," Bertrand suggested by way of a compromise.

"It's certainly distinctive," Christian chimed in.

"It's that, all right. But do farmers and bakers need distinctive?" Bertrand mused.

By now my father had heard enough. "Yes!" he snapped irritably. "They deserve to have something of their own. Something that says they may be farmers or bakers or postmen, but they are also French citizens who are proud of their country and will fight to defend it."

I hadn't seen my father this fired up in months—years, even. The old forest creature was crashing through the undergrowth again.

"I may be Italian," he continued triumphantly, "but the style of this car will be uniquely French! And by my honor, if there is a war, it just might win it for us!"

With that, he turned and strode toward the workshop, his head held high, as if he were a conquering general.

For a moment no one spoke. I'm not sure any of us fully understood what my father meant, but his words were rousing nonetheless.

Finally Bertrand turned to me. "What do you think?"

"Me?" I asked, thrown.

"Of course. The entire project is your doing. You must have the final say."

I looked at the car, searching for an answer. There was no doubting it: it did look uncannily like a duck crossed with a tin snail. But it had something else too—something I couldn't quite put my finger on. Then I got it.

It had attitude.

"I love it," I declared at last.

"Very well," Bertrand concluded. "Then there isn't a moment to lose." He turned to an astonished Christian. "We must go into production as soon as possible. Otherwise we won't have a factory left to build it in!"

"B-but the suspension . . . ," Christian stammered. "We haven't tested it yet. What if the car blows up like the last one?"

"Then you'd better test it quickly," Bertrand told him gruffly. "Because one way or another, the Tin Snail is going into production. Call me as soon as your tests are complete." With that, he turned and stalked back to his car.

Christian and I were speechless. We turned and surveyed the strange little car sitting in front of us, bolted together out of odd panels and parts salvaged from the wrecked car in the river.

True, it had a certain quirky charm. But quite how it was going to win a war was completely beyond me.

18 Double or Quits

Victor brought a tray of lagers over to the table and settled down to join our poker game.

It was two days since Bertrand had issued his ultimatum, and Christian and my father had been working on the car night and day. If Christian had been unsure about my father's styling, that was forgotten now. All that mattered was making sure that the new suspension system worked perfectly.

Christian had arrived at the bar an hour or so before, dripping with sweat from an unusually humid evening in the workshop. During the winter months it was like a fridge, offering precious little protection from the icy blasts from the north. Now, as the first really hot days of summer were upon us, the workshop had become a metal oven. Opening the doors would have helped, but Bertrand had insisted on total secrecy. So we had been forced to endure rocketing temperatures.

As he pulled up a chair and joined us, Christian looked exhausted. He still wasn't entirely happy with the suspension system and had spent the day painstakingly tweaking it. But it was too late and he was too tired to do any more tonight. Tomorrow would be another day.

Two hours later, the game was still going strong; it was all I could do to keep my eyes open. Even with the doors wide-open, the air in the bar felt stale and heavy. Piled up on the table in front of us was a mound of dog-eared notes—easily our largest "pot" yet.

Having spent most of the evening grumbling over his poor hands, my father now seemed confident that he was on to a winner. Sneaking a glance over his shoulder, I saw that he already had two queens. Another queen was sitting faceup in the center of the scuffed table.

One card was yet to be revealed. If it was a queen, my father would have four, an all-but-invincible hand. But if, by a stroke of almost unimaginable luck, Victor was concealing under his squat, hairy fingers the king of clubs, he would have a royal flush—the highest hand possible. So high that in all the months I had lived in the village, I had never seen it.

Christian and then Félix folded, tossing their cards into the pile. Next up was Benoît. He threw in his cards, but like the others, he wasn't about to leave. Not till I had dealt the last card.

My father blinked slowly, his face a mask of calm that hid his tension. I knew there was much more at stake for him than the winnings. This was about reputation, but more than anything, it was about beating Victor.

Victor smiled at him, showing his nicotine-stained teeth. "Your call, I believe."

My father pushed all his remaining chips, coins and cash into the center.

"All in." He was gambling everything, or almost everything, as I was about to discover.

I watched closely as the smile faded from Victor's lips. In the background, Dominique had stopped clearing tables and was now watching closely like the rest of the locals.

With a nod from my father, I took the top card from the pack and discarded it as usual. The next would seal Papa's fate one way or the other. I slowly put it down next to the other three that lay faceup on the table.

It was all I could do not to punch the air. It was the queen of diamonds!

As my father spread his cards out on the table, a gasp went up from the assembled onlookers as they realized he had four queens.

All eyes were now on Victor as his stubby fingers picked up his cards and placed them on the table.

For a moment there was a murmur of confusion, and then a collective intake of breath. The unimaginable had happened. It was a royal flush—the highest possible hand.

I blinked repeatedly, as if my eyes were deceiving me, and craned closer to see. "It can't be. . . ," I breathed.

"I assure you it can," Victor purred as his face cracked into a broad grin.

My father remained rigidly still, numb with shock. The nigh-on-impossible had happened.

Victor began to scoop up all his winnings hungrily.

"I hope you'll give us a chance to win it back," Christian said, eyeing him with suspicion.

"Of course," he replied. "But not tonight. My luck can last only so long."

My father sat brooding as Victor rose to his feet, struggling to carry all his winnings.

"There is, of course, the matter of the bet you made with Angelo," Papa suddenly announced. As the bar fell silent, I darted an anxious look at him.

"You're ready to show us this new car of yours?" Victor asked, intrigued.

"Papa, no! It's too soon," I warned him.

Christian too was looking alarmed now. "Luca—we still need another day or two."

But my father wasn't listening. He was staring straight at Victor. "Double or quits?" he asked coldly.

As Victor raised a curious eyebrow, I grabbed my father's arm more urgently. "We haven't finished all the tests."

Victor smiled smugly. "Maybe you should listen to your boy. Even he seems to have no faith in it."

"It's ready," Papa insisted, betraying a flicker of anger.

"Please, don't do this," I begged.

"You should have a little more faith in your own invention," he said determinedly. "I'm telling you, we're ready."

"And when would you like to complete your challenge?" Victor asked.

My father rose from his chair. "How about now?"

Christian and I stared at him in disbelief.

"You're a fool, Luca," Christian hissed, before striding furiously out of the bar.

I felt suddenly torn. I didn't want to see Victor win; but even less did I want Papa to make a fool of himself.

He must have sensed my conflict, and put an arm on my shoulder. "Trust me. We can win. Now, am I driving or are you?"

By the time we reached the test track, Victor and almost the entire village were already there. They had gathered in the field with a motley collection of oil lamps and flaming torches.

Marguerite was also there, her head swathed in a scarf tied under her bristly chin. As my father and I approached, she pushed Benoît toward us and he hobbled over.

"My wife would like you to know that we'd be happy to drive the car for you—for the test," he stuttered, before coughing up a large gobbet of mucus, which he spat onto the grass.

"That's very decent of you, Benoît," my father replied, touched by the old man's gesture. "So you know how to drive a car, then?"

"Haven't got a clue." He shrugged, his face cracking into a gummy grin. "But I'm a quick learner."

Before my father could take him up on his offer, I interrupted anxiously. "Christian isn't here."

"He'll come," Papa assured me. "He won't miss this."

Suddenly the crowd parted and Victor emerged into the center of the circle.

"So," he boomed, looking around theatrically. "Where is this wonderful new invention of yours? I'm sure we're all dying to see it."

On cue, the doors of the workshop were pulled open with a rusty groan that announced the appearance of the prototype. As the Tin Snail rattled out, the light from its single headlamp throbbed weakly in time with the engine.

A howl of laughter immediately went up from the assembled villagers.

"This is what you've been secretly building all these months?" Victor chuckled, eyeing the battered corrugated iron and the single windscreen wiper. I felt my cheeks immediately burn with indignation. "Tell me"—he turned to Benoît with more than a hint of mockery—"would you buy one?"

Benoît looked startled to be put on the spot in front of his neighbors. "Reckon by the look of it, I could make one myself," he wheezed. His remark was met by more gales of laughter and he smiled a toothless grin at finding himself suddenly so popular.

"I would," came a voice no one recognized.

Everyone looked around, wondering who had spoken.

"Who said that?" Victor demanded.

After a moment, Marguerite summoned the courage to step forward. "I did."

Her remark was met by a chorus of gasps. In over twenty years, not one of the villagers had heard her speak.

Benoît's wrinkled, prune-like eyes widened in disbelief. "M-Marguerite?" he stammered.

"Yes. That's right," she said, "I found my voice." She turned to me. "If your car will drive me to market so my excuse for a husband can stay working in the fields instead of lazing on his bony backside—then, yes, I will buy your car. I have enough put away."

Benoît looked astonished. "Since when?"

"There's a lot you don't know about me," she replied.

As the crowd of onlookers burst into laughter again, Benoît blinked uncertainly, not knowing how to handle this affront.

"Well, young Angelo"—Victor nodded—"you have your first customer. But I think before any money changes hands, we must see the goods. The proof of this particular pudding," he said, "is in the driving."

He turned to my father.

"I believe the rules of the bet call for a farmer and his wife to drive the car carrying two chickens, a jug of wine and a dozen eggs—am I right?" He turned back to the crowd. "Since Benoît can't drive, who here is willing to be our farmer?"

"I will," Camille declared, suddenly stepping forward. "I will be your farmer."

I glanced up and saw that she was looking straight at me. My heart was pounding inside my chest as I cleared my throat. "And I will be the driver," I announced.

"Strictly speaking, the rules call for a farmer and wife," Victor observed. "But I suppose if these two fine young people are willing to pretend, it's good enough for me."

"Then let's not waste any more time," my father declared. "One lap of the field, agreed?"

"Agreed." Victor beamed, clearly convinced he was set to double his winnings.

As my father put the flagon of wine in the back, I clambered nervously into the driver's seat and gripped the steering wheel. Was I really about to do this?

A moment later, the passenger door creaked open and Camille climbed in beside me holding a tray of eggs.

"Just so you know," she said, eyeing me defiantly, "if you crash this like last time, I'll kill you."

It was clearly intended as a joke, but by now my nerves were starting to get the better of me. Suddenly my father was at the window, craning to speak to me through the flap.

"No heroics, you understand? If anything—anything—goes wrong, get out. Forget the bet, do you hear me?"

"It won't go wrong," I assured him. But inside, my pulse was like machine-gun fire.

Marguerite squeezed two of her hens in through the passenger window and Camille clamped an arm firmly round each before turning to face me.

"You're sure you can handle this?"

I nodded and swallowed hard. "Whatever you do, just keep hold of those eggs. If one of them breaks, I'll hold you personally responsible."

For a second she must have thought I was serious; then her mouth slowly creased into a smile.

In front of us, lit up by the feeble headlamp, was a checkered flag one of the villagers had made out of a tea towel and a branch. Beyond that the ruts of the field receded into inky darkness.

I squeezed the floor pedal to set a little fuel and the engine slowly responded, rising to a whine that made the windows rattle and the speedometer go into spasm.

My father called to me above the noise. "Slow and steady."

I nodded, my mouth dry with anticipation. This was no longer just about winning a bet. Bertrand's unswerving faith, my father's career and, more than anything, my parents' marriage—all rested on the little car passing this test without disintegrating. Failure was simply not an option.

The checkered tea towel was waved and I eased out the clutch—a little too eagerly, as it happened. The car juddered forward, coming within a hairsbreadth of stalling. Luckily for my pride, it found its feet again and began to pick up a little speed.

Carefully, tentatively, I guided it toward the center of the plowed field. Beside me, Camille clutched the hens so tightly she was in danger of throttling them.

Both of us barely dared to breathe as the first of the ruts loomed in front of us in the dim headlight. Too slow, and I risked losing momentum and getting stuck. Too fast, and I could put too much strain on the suspension. Anything but the smallest jolt could make an egg tumble or send the hens into a flap.

The front wheels finally reached the first rut. For a moment the car ballooned upward and my heart gave a surge of fear as I waited for the back end to strike the ground. Would the suspension cope or would the car bottom out and snap the axle?

The answer came soon enough. Like a tiny schooner floating over a wave, the Tin Snail glided over the rut, then eased itself effortlessly down the other side.

"It's working!" I exclaimed. I allowed my foot to press the accelerator a little harder and the car began to pick up speed.

Camille began to tense again. Some of the eggs were starting to rattle. "Aren't we going too fast?"

But I was in my element, willing the car forward. "We need to reach thirty, otherwise the test-drive doesn't count."

This was one of Bertrand's golden rules. But by now the hens were becoming increasingly afflicted by motion sickness and fighting to get free.

"You have to slow down," Camille called out as the car continued to barrel over the plowed field.

"Just a little more," I urged, squinting to see through the windscreen, which was now caked in mud thrown up by the tires. I glanced down, frantically groping for the windscreen wiper.

"I can't see!" I cried. "Work the wiper."

"I can't!" Camille shouted. "The hens . . ." She was desperately fighting to contain the birds.

Unable to see, we suddenly hit a deep, rocky gulley near the edge of the field. To my amazement, the eggs still didn't break, but a deafening crunch of metal announced a far more serious problem.

"The brakes!" I shouted, pounding the floor with my foot. "They're broken!"

I'd barely got the words out before the car slammed through a fence and began to plunge down the hillside beyond, scattering rabbits in every direction.

Suddenly a pair of fox eyes was staring back at me dead ahead. Yanking the steering wheel hard to the right, I narrowly avoided colliding with a tree, only to discover that a much larger obstacle was now looming straight ahead of us.

"Get down!" I screamed, and we dived behind the dashboard just in time as we went headlong into Benoît's barn. The wooden doors exploded around us like shrapnel, and the Tin Snail careered through a pile of rusty farm machinery before embedding itself in a very large bale of straw.

Camille spat out some straw and pulled several twigs from her hair before blinking away the mud that was by now evenly coating her face. Next to her, I sat rigid in shock.

"Well, by and large, I'd say that went pretty well," I concluded.

"This is what you call 'pretty well'?" she asked, staring around at the barn incredulously.

"But it worked!" I cried, my eyes shining with excitement. "The suspension worked."

Camille stared at me, then calmly cracked an egg on my forehead. The gooey yolk trickled down my face till it ran over my mouth and I licked it away with my tongue.

"I'm going to leave now," she said, and reached for the door handle. But this was easier said than done. Having sustained several glancing blows from fences and tree branches, the door refused to budge. But one swift kick with the heel of her boot sent it clanking to the ground.

Quick release, I thought, making a mental note.

Within minutes the villagers began to arrive to survey the carnage. First on the scene was my father. He rushed down the hillside toward Camille.

"Are you all right?" he panted.

"Oh, fine," Camille answered sarcastically. "In fact, apparently everything went pretty well."

There was a loud rasp of metal as I levered the driver's

door open. My father rushed over to me, hauling me free from the wreckage.

"Are you OK? Did you break anything?"

"Only the headlamp," I replied with a rueful smile. "Oh, and the brake pipe kind of snapped back there somewhere."

"Who cares about the car. I meant you," he said. "I thought for a moment . . ." He trailed off, unable to utter the words.

"I'm fine. The main thing is, we won." I beamed.

"What are you talking about? Of course we didn't. The car's a write-off."

"No, you don't understand," I protested. "The eggs. Look at them."

Papa glanced at the tray of eggs Camille, astonishingly, was still holding. Apart from the one she'd broken on my head, they were all, miraculously, still in one piece. What's more, the flagon of wine was intact.

For a second my father struggled to take in the enormity of what he was seeing. Then, slowly, his mouth spread into a smile and he pulled me clean off my feet.

"Angelo! You did it!"

As he hugged me ecstatically, I glanced back at Camille to see that, despite herself, even she was smiling. As our eyes met, I suddenly felt a scalding sensation down the back of my neck. I wasn't sure if it was whiplash, excitement at finally fulfilling Bertrand's brief, or because I realized that, despite all her protests to the contrary, Camille really didn't hate me after all.

In fact, it was just possible we might finally be friends.

19 Sunday, September 3, 1939

"You've heard, I assume?" Bertrand asked, looking white as a sheet.

"Just now," my father replied. "It was all over the newspapers when we got into the station."

Two hours earlier, at precisely five p.m., the French government had followed the British and declared war on Hitler's Germany.

It was three days after I'd crashed the prototype into Benoît's barn, and my father and I had traveled up to Paris to tell Bertrand the brilliant news about the suspension in person. We'd wanted to come up sooner, but the day after the test run there had been ominous news: Germany had invaded Poland. This was a direct challenge to Britain and France, who had vowed to defend Poland.

Had Germany been calling their bluff or deliberately goading them into war? Either way, our worst fears had become a reality. We were now at war.

We'd made our way to Paris as fast as we could, but it wasn't easy. The threat of imminent war had caused havoc to the trains. Those services that hadn't been canceled were piled full of people urgently traveling back to Paris or fleeing to the countryside.

By the time we finally reached the city, it was buzzing with the news we were dreading.

"What does it mean for the car?" I asked cautiously.

Bertrand's face was somber. "It means we're too late."

"But we did your test," I pleaded. "We drove over the field without breaking the eggs."

"I'm pleased. But now you must scrap everything."

My father gasped. "What? But surely—"

"Listen to me. Go back to the village. Find every trace of the prototypes—petrol cans, starter motors, the lot—then destroy them."

"Destroy them?" I repeated, hardly believing my ears.

"You can't mean that," Papa protested.

"Nothing must be left." Bertrand was staring wildly, more agitated than ever. "Promise me."

"But—but why?" I stammered. "After everything we've done . . ."

"Because the only thing worse than destroying that little car is the Germans finding it. And if they invade, that's exactly what they'll try to do."

Things were moving too fast for me. Bertrand could clearly see the thoughts crowding into my head and stepped closer.

"There's no need to be afraid," he said, looking into my eyes earnestly. "We will win this war eventually, of that I am certain. But one thing is essential: the Germans must never, never discover those prototypes."

"Now listen to me," my father growled angrily. "I never wanted to make this car in the first place, but you convinced me that it was the right thing to do. And I believed you." His eyes were burning like molten lead. "Building that car from scratch has been the hardest—and the proudest— achievement of my career, and no blasted German army is going to destroy that! I've—we've—come too far for that."

"Papa," I said softly, gripping his arm. "Bertrand's right. If we don't break up the cars, the Germans will steal everything. We can build it again in a few months once the war is over."

"We have no idea how long this war will last—anything could have happened by then," he protested. "Besides, what would we build it from? We've made no blueprints of the new design."

"None at all?" Bertrand asked, alarmed.

"We didn't have time," Papa explained. "Everything is up here." He pointed vaguely to his head.

But Bertrand was immovable. The cars had to be destroyed to prevent them falling into enemy hands.

"If there was any other way . . ." He sighed sadly.

For a moment my father was completely still; then, with one violent movement of his arm, he swept everything off Bertrand's desk. It smashed against the wall, making me start. He stood there for a moment, breathing hard, trying to steady his nerves.

"I'm sorry," he said eventually, his voice catching with emotion. "It's just such a blasted waste."

✿

An hour later, with only seconds to spare, we clambered onto the train back to Regnac and found the last remaining seats. We were lucky to get them—the train was filling up with families taking their children away to the relative safety of the country. War had been declared only a matter of hours earlier, but already people were terrified German bombs would start raining down from the sky or the streets would echo to the march of jackboots.

As our train rumbled out of the station, my father and I sat in stunned silence. Eventually my fear got the better of me.

"Maman won't be able to come back now, will she?" I said.

My father sighed heavyheartedly and shook his head. "No," he muttered. "Italy is on Germany's side. Even if she could get back into the country, she wouldn't be welcome here."

I felt like I'd been stabbed through the side.

"What about you?" I asked, scared now. "Will they hurt you?"

He turned to me, frowning. "Hurt me?"

"Because you're Italian."

For a moment he looked grave; then his face softened. "No. They won't hurt me."

"How can you be so sure?"

He smiled, all trace of his earlier outburst gone. "Haven't you heard? I'm Luca Fabrizzi, father of Angelo, the creator of the Tin Snail. How could the people of France possibly hurt me?" he said, his eyes shining with pride.

I was curled up on the seat, fast asleep, when my father gently shook me by the shoulder.

"We're here."

I got to my feet awkwardly. One of my legs had fallen asleep and was now throbbing with pins and needles. I hobbled after my father and climbed down onto the platform. When I looked up, I saw Christian waiting for us.

"I thought you might have left already," Papa ventured cautiously. Even though the test-drive had technically been a success, he knew that Christian was still furious with him for "gambling" with the car before it was finished.

"I was going to leave," Christian replied. "But then Bertrand rang me." He didn't look angry anymore—just grim. "I guess we have work to do."

As soon as we got back to the village, we headed straight for the bar to discuss our next move. Camille was nowhere to be seen, but I'd heard some of the older villagers discussing a heated argument between Victor and Philippe.

Philippe wanted to sign up for the army and go to the front line, but his father had forbidden him to even try. He would find some other way for his son to serve his country, he had been overheard shouting. Enraged, Philippe had shut himself away in his room, refusing to come out for days.

The mood in the bar was tense. A few locals were huddled round the radio, listening to government broadcasts about what was happening with Germany while we took our usual table by the door.

"There has to be another way," Christian sighed as he slumped down in his seat. "After all this work, to simply destroy everything . . ."

"If you can think of one, tell us," my father said, scowling.

"What about the Paris Motor Show?" Christian asked him anxiously.

"What motor show? There won't be one." He ground his pistachio shell into the table testily.

"The important thing is that the Nazis don't find it," I insisted.

"You mean Ferdinand Porsche," my father muttered. "You're assuming he even knows about the car—let alone this village."

"Angelo's got a point," Christian told him. "If Bertrand's right, he's already got his spies looking everywhere. It won't take them long to work out that Bertrand used to test cars here."

My father looked like he was going to argue, then changed his mind. "Fine," he said, pushing his chair back with a determined scrape. "Then, if we have no choice, we do it now. Tonight."

"But where?" I shrugged.

Papa thought for a moment. "In the barn."

"The one we crashed into?" I asked skeptically. "What if Benoît won't let us?"

"Then we don't tell him," he replied with a mischievous glint in his eye.

Less than an hour later, Christian, my father and I had driven the last of the prototypes down to the barn. Two of the mock-ups were barely roadworthy, but luckily the route from the workshop, as I knew only too well, was almost entirely downhill.

Christian took charge of the proceedings.

"Break them up into the smallest parts you can—the smaller the better. Then bury them around the barn. No one will notice them amongst all the other rusty junk."

I looked at the vehicles doubtfully. "There's no way we can bury all this."

"We've got no choice," Christian insisted.

Suddenly I heard a noise and froze. "Listen."

"What is it?" my father whispered. Christian put a finger to his lips and crept to the door.

At first there was nothing. Then we all saw at once.

Across the field, three figures were approaching with oil lamps swaying in the darkness.

"Who is it?" I asked, unnerved.

Christian looked closely; then his face fell. "Victor," he hissed.

"What does he want?" my father said, and cursed.

We would know soon enough. After a few moments Victor approached the door to the barn. He was accompanied by Benoît and Félix.

"Ah, Victor . . ." My father smiled, trying to appear casual. "Have you come to settle the bet we won the other night?"

"Forget the bet," Victor barked. His mood had changed. His usual smug sneer had vanished. "You've come to bury the cars," he said accusingly. "Don't bother denying it. I overheard."

My heart sank.

"What's it to you if we have?" Papa asked coldly.

Benoît stepped forward. "Last time I checked, this was my barn," he muttered with a little flicker of cunning at the corner of his mouth.

My father returned the smile. "My mistake. We'll go else-where."

He made to leave, but Victor stepped in front of him to block his exit. "I don't think so," he growled.

My father eyed him closely, trying to read him.

Christian quickly stepped between them, all smiles. "Is there a problem?" he asked in a conciliatory manner.

Victor turned to him slowly and gave him a hard stare. "Your cars are the problem."

"What about them?" my father asked, his eyes flinty with hate now.

Victor turned back to him and looked thoughtful. "They're for French people, yes?"

Papa looked at him, a little thrown by the question. "Yes, but—"

"Then no German soldier is getting his hands on them," Victor told him defiantly.

For a second I couldn't believe my ears. "Wait a minute. You—you're here to help us?" I stammered.

"You can't bury them all in my barn, can you?" Benoît grinned, gums peeling back to show his two rotten pegs.

Christian, my father and I glanced at each other with incredulous smiles.

"Trust me," Victor assured us, "the cars will be much harder to find if we scatter the parts around the whole village."

"But what if the Germans find out you've helped us?" I blurted.

"Angelo's right," Christian said. "You could be killed."

It was Félix's turn to speak. "That is why everyone will do their part. That way we are all guilty."

I couldn't believe what I was hearing. "You'd do this for us?"

Victor looked at me, astonished. "Absolutely not." He sniffed. "We do it for France."

Benoît pulled his creaky old back as upright as he could manage. "Some of us are too old or too young to fight in the war. But this is one way we can do something," he announced proudly.

Astonished, Papa stepped forward and thrust out his hand. For a moment Victor looked at it uncertainly; then he shook it firmly.

"Together we stand," my father declared.

"Together," came back six voices in unison.

Within the hour, almost every inhabitant of the village was crammed into the bar in the main square. Those who couldn't fit in spilled out onto the pavement, jostling and craning to listen. A scruffy little boy of no more than six whose mother took in washing scurried under the legs of those in front to feed news to stragglers at the back.

Victor climbed unsteadily onto a chair to address the

impromptu gathering. He'd put his waistcoat on over his braces, and was now wearing a pair of small, academic-looking glasses. This normally signified that he was on important municipal business. He cleared his throat and the congregation finally fell silent.

"As elected mayor of this parish, with all the incumbent powers and responsibilities vested in me by my office—" he began stuffily. Almost immediately his speech was derailed by a heckler at the back.

"Get on with it, you pompous old windbag!"

A loud guffaw of laughter went up from the crowd, and Victor snatched off his glasses and scowled toward the back of the room to see who the culprit was. After a moment the laughter subsided and he indignantly returned the glasses to his nose. He cleared his throat and continued where he'd left off.

"We are a proud people," he continued, more briskly this time. "None more so than the citizens of this village. As I look amongst you I am proud to be called not just your mayor, but—I hope—your friend." There were one or two raised eyebrows around the room, and for a moment Victor's smile faltered. He gave his forehead a quick dab with his handkerchief and pushed on.

"As you all know, some time ago a group of people, friends of Monsieur Hipaux, came to stay in our village. They're standing here tonight at my side."

I felt suddenly self-conscious as, one by one, everyone's gaze fell on me.

"I think it's fair to say that many of us were suspicious when they first arrived," Victor declared. "Myself included.

Too often the rural backbone of this country has been ignored by the so-called elite from the cities, as if we don't
exist."

I glanced up at my father, alarmed at where this train
of thought was leading. Victor was obviously starting to get
into his stride now.

"But it is the good people of this village, and hundreds
just like us the length and breadth of this country, who keep
this nation alive, put food on its tables and clothes in its
shops. Without us, all those fine fellows in their fancy cars
and palatial homes would cease to exist. . . ."

Victor suddenly hesitated, sensing he was getting carried
away.

"As I was saying"—he smiled awkwardly—"even I had
my doubts about their motives. But I stand before you now
a changed man, because these people didn't come here to
make some luxury car to sell at their fancy motor show. They
came here to make a car for us. For the working man . . ."

I saw Victor's eye alight on the stony face of Marguerite,
scowling up at him. "And woman," he added hastily. "It may
not look like much," he continued. "In fact, it looks like a
heap of junk. . . ." I wasn't sure whether to raise an objec-
tion to this, but decided against it as Victor pressed on. "But
it's ours. The car these people have designed is going to put
villages like ours back on the map, where they belong."

Suddenly his voice took on a darker tone. "But be sure of
one thing: all this will have been for nothing unless we stop
the enemy in its tracks."

His voice rang out through the room like a hammer strik-
ing an anvil.

"This war is about our freedom, about our right to be who we are. And nothing symbolizes that more than the car we all witnessed up in that field. That car is our freedom. It is everything this country has ever stood for. And if it falls into the enemy's hands—and make no mistake, they will come looking for it—then the war will already have been lost."

For a moment there was silence in the bar. Victor had surpassed himself with his stirring call to arms. But had it worked? Would the villagers be willing to risk everything for the sake of the Tin Snail?

Having found her voice at last, Marguerite was the first to speak up.

"So what do you suggest we do? Throw bread at them?"

A titter of amusement ran through the bar.

"I dare say one of your loaves could wipe out half an armored division," Victor snorted, making Marguerite's jaw tighten like steel.

"What I suggest," he continued quickly, "is something far simpler. We help them destroy the cars."

The room descended into confusion and Victor raised his voice above the hubbub. "I will be dividing all of you up into groups. Each group will then be responsible for taking away one of the prototypes and dismantling it into the smallest pieces possible. Nothing—I repeat, nothing—must be left behind. Every nut, bolt and screw must be hidden as far and wide as possible."

Within the hour something resembling a strange-looking crew was striding toward Benoît's barn, armed with spanners, hammers, hacksaws and just about every farm implement they could lay their hands on at a moment's notice.

"Just think," Christian said, turning to me wryly. "This way we get to win the war and stick it to Ferdinand the Fritz."

Within minutes the villagers had descended on the prototypes like packs of dogs, wheeling them away and stripping them to the bone—or crankshaft. Several of the larger items wouldn't need much disguising at all—they were simply returned to their original homes. So Félix got many of his blacksmith's tools back; some he hadn't even realized had gone missing. Several items also found their way back into Bertrand's scullery, including a large washboard, a bucket and an assortment of kitchen utensils.

I was due to help my father and Christian with the task of dismantling the final prototype—the only successful model and the most vital to hide. But Victor and his small band of villagers were struggling with the one Bertrand and I had blown up in the top field several months earlier. One of the wheels had dropped off, and much of the undercarriage had been scorched to a cinder when the magnesium caught fire.

"Angelo," my father called across to me, "why don't you help Victor?"

For a moment I was unsure. Perhaps part of me was still getting used to the idea of Victor as a comrade. Helping him would also mean working alongside Philippe, who had now reluctantly joined us. After his remarks about Camille, I still wasn't ready to forgive him, even if we were all on the same side now. But I was keen to make sure that every single prototype was properly broken up.

My father must have seen my hesitation.

"Go. Christian and I will take care of this."

"I'll help you," Camille offered, coming over to join me.

"You're not still angry with me?" I asked. It had been only three days since I'd crashed the car into the barn. Maybe I'd imagined that she had started to like me.

"Yes," she said matter-of-factly. "But at least this way you won't be able to take me on any more test-drives."

I left my father and Christian to deal with the latest prototype and set off after Camille to help the others.

Some time later we descended on the graveyard next to the church armed with pickaxes and spades. Victor had hit on the novel idea of burying some of our car parts in an old grave.

"Shouldn't we ask someone first?" I ventured.

"I'm the mayor," he announced. "What more permission do you need?"

I saw Philippe smirk to himself, pleased to see me put in my place.

Soon we were all busily digging and picking away at the grave. Suddenly, round the back of the church, a door opened and the pastor, a timid and sickly young man called Grévoul, who had only recently been ordained, came scurrying out, his nightclothes billowing in the breeze. It turned out that he'd been called away to Boutonne on parish business and had missed the meeting. The sight of a group of men digging up a grave clearly filled him with terror.

"Stop! Stop!" he hollered as he raced across the cemetery, the breeze whistling around his ankles. "What do you think you're doing?"

Even when Victor had managed to calm him down and explain that we were not grave robbers but on top-secret municipal business, he looked deeply uneasy. But Victor was in his stride now. As the pastor watched, ghostlike in his nightshirt, we resumed our digging. Soon our spades clunked against the wood of the old coffin.

The pastor clutched a handkerchief to his mouth in horror. "Please tell me you don't intend to open it!"

"We don't need to." Victor beamed, the gold fillings in his teeth glinting in the moonlight. "We're going to hide everything underneath, then put the coffin back on top."

The pastor smiled falteringly. I was sure he was close to fainting, but his knees held out long enough for him to see an assortment of gear cogs, crankshafts and gaskets safely posted under the coffin and the earth shoveled back on top.

For tonight, at least, our work was done. Now all we had to do was sit back and hope the Germans didn't come after all.

20 1:46

After Victor had calmed the pastor's nerves with a little brandy, I returned to the manor house. To my surprise, Christian was already back, stowing a suitcase in his latest sports car.

"You're leaving?" I asked, confused.

"I have to," he replied. "My mother is terrified there'll be an invasion, so I promised I'd get back to Paris and help her pack up."

"But what about the prototype?"

"Don't worry about that," he assured me. "Your father is out there now, stripping it down to the last nut. I wouldn't wait up for him. He's going to be a while yet."

"I should go and help him," I said, turning to head back out of the gates.

"You won't find him," Christian insisted. "He's determined to spread every part as far and wide as possible. He could be miles away. Get some sleep. He'll be back by morning."

He threw the last of his things into the car before planting a reassuring hand on my shoulder.

"I'll see you up in Paris in a few days, OK?" he said, painting on a positive smile.

I nodded, suddenly feeling a cloud of despair descend on me.

He must have sensed it because he pulled me into his arms and gave me a fierce embrace. "You mustn't worry," he said. "With any luck we'll have kicked these Germans back where they belong before the month's out." But I could see that he believed it even less than I did.

"It's not just that," I sighed. "It's everything. This car was going to make things all right again. Now they're worse than ever."

Christian fixed me with a stern look. "What does Bertrand always say? Some things aren't meant to be. The rest aren't meant to be yet."

"You think something good can come of this?" I asked in disbelief. "Everything we've worked on is in pieces, two meters under the ground."

Christian gently raised my chin with his finger. "Your idea was brilliant. And one day it will take the world by storm. Just not yet. Now get some sleep and I'll see you in Paris."

Moments later I watched the sports car churn up the gravel as Christian roared out of the courtyard onto the bumpy track outside. I listened to it clatter its way down the hillside and up the other side to the village until it was finally gone.

For a while all was silent; then a fox cried somewhere far off in the night—probably the one I'd narrowly missed. I wondered if my father could hear it too as he buried the last remnants of the Tin Snail, possibly forever.

In the stillness of the night, I found it hard to comprehend that somewhere just beyond the French border, bombs might already be falling.

Several hours later I was huddled under a blanket in Bertrand's study when I was woken by a gentle nudge on my shoulder. It was my father. As I stirred from my sleep, I saw that his face was covered in dirt.

"Sorry I took so long. I thought Christian would tell you to go to bed."

"He did. But I wanted to see you. Is it done?" I asked breathlessly.

He nodded gravely. "Nothing's left."

"You're sure they won't be able to find it?"

"Trust me. Even if they find one part of it, they'll never find all the others."

I wasn't sure whether to feel relieved or defeated. Both, I supposed. It felt like the end of an era. The end, in a funny sort of way, of my childhood.

The next couple of days were spent double-checking all the hiding places around the village. I was terrified someone had been slapdash—that a hiding place was too obvious, a well too shallow or a vegetable patch not replanted with turnips.

I needn't have worried. The villagers turned out to be

incredibly resourceful. Maybe, like Benoît, they'd had years of hiding illicit liquor stills from local officials.

By the end, no one would have known that for the last eight months or more, two famous car designers and a thirteen-year-old boy had been assembling a string of prototypes in a makeshift workshop.

Finally the time came for my father and me to follow Christian back to Paris.

Victor came out of his bar to see us off personally. Dominique joined him and presented us with a large cake tin. Inside was a selection of her finest confections, topped off by two frosted almond macaroons.

"In case your little pâtisserie in Paris is closed," she told me warmly. "Enjoy them while you can. They're saying chocolate could be rationed soon."

I saw my father shudder at the thought. I accepted the cake tin gratefully while, for the second time that week, Papa found himself shaking Victor's hand.

"Thank you for everything," he said. "We could never have done it without you."

"It was my honor," Victor said proudly, meaning every word. "And I haven't forgotten that I owe you those winnings from our bet. I always pay my debts."

"You have more than repaid any debts," my father told him. "Anyway, save them for when we come back to visit."

"So you'll definitely return?" Victor asked.

"Someone has to dig up all the car parts after the war," he quipped. "You don't think we were just going to leave them here?"

Victor gave a snort of laughter and the two men shook

hands again, all trace of their former animosity finally buried—along with the Tin Snail.

When we got back to Paris, I was able to speak to my mother again. For days it had proved impossible to put a call through to her remote Italian village, but eventually the phone rang in the little concierge's apartment in the lobby of our block. When I was handed the receiver, I heard Maman's anxious voice over the crackling line.

"Angelo, my darling, is that you?"

I felt a surge of joy and longing at hearing her after so long. I could tell that she was desperately trying not to cry. Suddenly the war seemed more real than ever. But what was worse, it almost felt like my mother was on the other side. She wasn't, of course—France was her adopted country now—but she was marooned in Italy. For how long was anyone's guess.

"How are you, my love?" she asked, frantic for all my news. "Are you going to school at all?" I darted a look at my father, struggling to remember what lie I was supposed to be telling about my education.

"Don't worry," she went on quickly. Her voice became hushed, more serious now. "Listen to me, Angelo. Your father is going to try and see if he can get you on a train to Italy. I'm not sure if it will be possible, my darling, but we have to try."

I threw a panicked glance at Papa. I missed my mother desperately—more than I ever thought I would—but leaving for Italy? The thought was unimaginable. I had to stay in France to protect the Tin Snail from the Germans at all costs.

My mother wasn't able to talk much more before she was cut off; just long enough to convey frantic information to my father. To my dismay, I overheard him giving her repeated assurances that he would do everything he could to arrange my train. No sooner had he hung up the receiver than I launched into an impassioned plea to stay. But before I could get more than two words in, he held up his hand to silence me.

"It's OK. I'm not going to send you to Italy."

"You—you're not?" I stuttered, taken aback.

"Perhaps if I could come with you . . ." He faltered. I could feel panic rising in my chest again. "But I can't," he continued, more defiant now. "France is our home. It took us in and gave us refuge, and I'm blasted if I'm going to desert it now."

I closed my eyes with relief. I desperately wanted to be reunited with my mother—for all three of us to be reunited—but saving the Tin Snail and France was simply more important.

Every morning, over the coming weeks and months, I took the métro with my father to the factory on the quayside. Paris was becoming almost unrecognizable now. With sandbags and barbed wire on every corner, it looked more like a fortress than a city.

Yet the strangest thing happened. At first, people panicked about the Germans sweeping over the border. Memories of the last war were still fresh in their minds. An entire generation of young men had been killed or maimed, and the prime minister and his cabinet were locked in furious disagreement over how best to prevent it happening again.

Some felt that we were more than ready to repel the enemy, while others insisted we were woefully unprepared.

But as the months passed, and with them my fourteenth birthday, no invasion came. So much so that people began to wonder if there really was a war at all.

Not Bertrand. He was convinced the Germans would come—and when they did, it would be fast and ruthless. After all, hadn't Ferdinand Porsche himself designed their tanks . . . the much-feared Panzers?

In the meantime, people carried on with their work much as they had before. Any issue about my father's job was completely forgotten as Bertrand put him to work designing the artillery trailers that the factory was now churning out.

At first there was a real sense of everyone pulling together for the war effort—even if there didn't seem to be an actual war. But slowly a new mood crept into the factory. I couldn't put my finger on it at first, but soon I knew exactly what it was.

Suspicion. Throughout France, foreigners were being rounded up, especially those from countries like Italy that were allied to the enemy. War was making everyone paranoid and jumpy. How long would it be before someone tipped off the authorities about my father?

During this time, nothing was said within the walls of the factory about the buried prototypes. It was far too risky. Any conversations were kept strictly between the four of us—me, Christian, my father and Bertrand—at Bertrand's home. But even there Bertrand would go through an elaborate sweep of the apartment to satisfy himself that we weren't being spied on.

Usually the conversation was brief. Occasionally a report surfaced of a dog unearthing one of the concealed parts in the village. My father seemed even more on edge than the rest of us. But after a number of lapses in security, all breaches had been sealed. The village was effectively in lockdown. It had quietly withdrawn itself from the outside world, hunkering down like a hedgehog going into hibernation, hoping that the rest of the world would quietly pass it by without noticing.

Christmas came and went, and then spring, yet still the Germans didn't come. Then, one crisp, sunny day, my father and I were emerging from the métro station on our way back from lunch when I felt a sudden crushing thump in my chest. A fraction of a second later there was a hissing suck of air and I was blasted clean off my feet.

Sprawling on the pavement, I looked up: ahead of us, a vast cloud of dust was mushrooming into the sky, raining debris and brickwork down onto the cars parked in the street. My ears were ringing and I could taste something acrid like sulfur in my mouth. As I tried to blink away the dust that was plastered over my face and eyes, I became aware of my father gently lifting me to my feet.

"Angelo! Are you all right?" His voice sounded eerie, like he was underwater, as I nodded, bewildered.

"What happened?"

"I think it was a bomb," he said. "Can you walk?"

I nodded again and he grabbed my hand. The next second we were running up the street. By now we had been joined by scores of others, all rushing in the same direction, their faces caked in white dust. As we approached the corner I felt a terrible dread rising in my chest; I already knew what lay round it.

But nothing could have prepared me for the sight that met my eyes as I finally rounded the bend. Where the factory should have been, there was now scarcely half a building left. A vast smoldering crater had taken its place.

I stopped dead in my tracks, unable to process what my eyes were telling me. All I could think of was Bertrand: when we had left for the station he had been in his office. Now it was completely gone. My father too stood paralyzed with shock and fear. A scalding wave of panic rose up inside me and my eyes were stinging with tears. But as I was about to take a step forward, I suddenly became aware of a figure standing beside me.

His glasses were cracked and covered in dust and his face was like a ghost's. But there was no mistaking who it was: Bertrand. He was even wearing his trusty trilby, though that was looking even more battered than usual.

"I thought you were . . ." I trailed off, unable to say the words.

"Dead? I'm afraid not." He smiled ruefully. "It was such a beautiful day, I went down to the river for a picnic."

As my father sighed with relief, I threw my arms around Bertrand and buried my face in the wool of his trench coat.

But there was no time for celebration. Others were still trapped in the rubble. Quick as a flash, we began sifting through it, frantically looking for survivors.

It was 1:46 in the afternoon when the German bomb struck the factory. But as luck would have it, it wasn't just Bertrand who'd gone out for a picnic. Thanks to a sudden break in the cold weather, almost all the workers were taking their lunch outside. Miraculously, the number of casualties was small.

The bomb had managed to miss the production line by about ten meters. Instead, it had destroyed the entire design department and offices.

But more alarmingly, it signaled imminent invasion by the German army—an invasion that would be so fast and ruthless it took the entire country by surprise.

A few days later my father and I were called into the makeshift office Bertrand had set up in the storeroom behind the canteen.

As he peered over his spectacles, his face looked even more woebegone than usual. "The time has come for you to leave," he told us darkly.

My father started to protest, but Bertrand held up a hand, adamant.

"We have had a very lucky escape, but we may not get another. The Germans are on our doorstep, and in their wake, Ferdinand Porsche will come, or at least his envoys."

"What will you do?" I asked anxiously.

"Stay here, of course," he replied bullishly. "Someone has to keep things running."

"But what's left to run?" my father protested. "The Germans will take over everything."

"Yes," Bertrand conceded. "But there is more than one way to fight this war. I'm too old to go to the front line, but I fully intend to fight . . . just from the inside."

"I don't understand." I frowned. "You're going to work for the Germans?"

"The Germans will almost certainly make us produce vehicles for their own war effort. Scout cars, trucks, that sort of thing."

I wasn't sure I was hearing this right. "You'd help them do that?"

"Absolutely," Bertrand declared, before adding slyly: "But I will make sure that they are the most unreliable, faulty vehicles ever produced by a car plant."

"It won't work," my father warned. "They'll figure you straightaway."

"I wouldn't be so sure," said Bertrand, with a devious smile. "Believe me, there are ways and means of wrecking a car without it being detected. In the meantime you must at all costs return to the village," he insisted. "Our German rivals aren't stupid. Very far from it. They almost certainly know we have been designing our own people's car. If they discover we've been using a secret test track near the house, it won't be long before they come looking."

"Will you come?" I asked.

"No," Bertrand replied firmly. "It will only attract more attention. It could be dangerous for the villagers. You will have to be my eyes and ears. Now go, both of you, while you still can."

Papa walked round the desk and gave him a huge bear hug. Bertrand held him tightly, a rare show of emotion. Then he turned to me.

"I'm relying on you," he told me. "And take care of Camille. The villagers may not be so kind to the daughter of a German now that the tide is turning."

My father put his hand on my shoulder and steered me

gently toward the door. Before I left I glanced back. Bertrand was looking out the window, lost in thought. For a moment he was quite still, his face suddenly older than I remembered. The lines around his eyes cast deep shadows where they were etched across his skin.

Suddenly, without warning, the sun appeared from behind the clouds and rebounded off his glasses, making them flash like liquid silver. Like a pair of welder's goggles, in fact. Then, as suddenly as it had come, the light was gone, almost as if someone had thrown a switch.

21 Invasion

If people hadn't believed there was a real war before, they were no longer in any doubt now. German tanks were chewing up the French countryside at a furious pace.

France was taken completely by storm. The air force tried to scramble its fighter planes into the sky, but the German Stukas—two-man dive-bombers—were far faster, and destroyed half of them before they had even left the ground.

Before long the French army was in full-scale retreat. But the German Panzers were so fast, French soldiers were falling back to villages that had already been captured by the Germans.

There were some truly astonishing acts of bravery—particularly by France's elite cavalry, which confronted the Germans in battle despite facing overwhelming odds.

But before long entire regiments were surrendering and being taken prisoner. In the space of weeks, nearly two million of France's population had been captured, many of them shipped off to German prisoner-of-war camps. More would follow; both towns and countryside were decimated. Those soldiers who weren't taken prisoner simply melted back into the local population and fled south as fast as they could.

On June 14 the German army roared into the streets of Paris. By midday, the swastika had been run up the flagpole at the city hall and Germany was officially in control.

Within days, panic had seized the country as rumors spread of the atrocities carried out by the Germans. According to some, the German secret police were even chopping off the hands of schoolboys to stop them becoming soldiers.

Hundreds of thousands fled, grabbing their most prized possessions and ramming them into any form of transport they could find. The roads out of the city were soon clogged with columns of evacuees fleeing south, carrying everything from mattresses to birdcages. Thriving cities and villages were reduced to ghost towns, the streets full of pets roaming around, abandoned.

It wasn't just pets either. Children were being parted from their parents in the panicked crushes at train stations. Seats were so hard to come by, some parents were simply shoving their children onto any passing train in the hope of keeping them safe.

But despite all this, after a few weeks a new rumor slowly began to drift in on the breeze. The invading army might not be the evil brutes we had been led to believe. Instead of plundering, they were being polite and paying for the goods they needed—sometimes well over the asking price. In some places they were even handing out free chocolate and ice cream!

If this was the invading army, maybe occupation wasn't so bad after all. At least, that was what some were starting to say.

Not Papa. He was resolute. It was all just a German publicity stunt to make people give up without a shot being fired. Besides, we'd already had more than a taste of what the enemy was capable of at the factory.

Whatever my father thought, within days of the invasion there was already talk of a cease-fire. Germany had promised that France would be allowed to carry on much as usual—in exchange for paying its new occupiers a hefty slice of its income.

To many it seemed like a good deal. Especially if it avoided any unnecessary bloodshed. But if the rest of the country was giving in, the little village of Regnac had no such intention.

On the day we arrived back there, we interrupted a small ceremony in the main square. Victor was dressed up in his finest flannel suit, carrying out the ritual with as much pomp as he could muster. Many of the locals had also dressed up to observe. Even Benoît wore his Sunday suit and a freshly pressed shirt.

As we stood watching, the flag above Victor's bar, the tricolore, was carefully lowered. Then, rather than being folded up, it was ceremonially burned, right there in front of everyone.

It was a shocking sight. Even Félix, who rarely showed

any emotion, wiped a tear away from his eye as Benoît put a comforting arm round Marguerite, who sobbed quietly.

I couldn't believe what I was seeing.

"How can you just stand here and let Victor do this?" I asked Félix, astonished.

"Better the flag is burned," he answered solemnly, "than that it should be disgraced by falling into enemy hands."

Suddenly I understood. This was no betrayal of France's most precious symbol of freedom. This was open defiance. Nothing could be worse than the German invaders taking our prized flag, as they had done in Paris.

But of course, Regnac had something else to protect— the knowledge that it, and it alone, was responsible for safeguarding the prototypes for the little Tin Snail. The Germans might have overthrown our country, but they— and, more to the point, Ferdinand Porsche—would never get their hands on them.

As I looked around, I noticed that two people were missing. Camille and Philippe.

It wasn't until the following day that I ran into them.

Victor had decreed that the young people left in the village must continue their schooling, regardless of the imminent threat. Life would continue just as before—as far as it could, anyway.

One small fly in this ointment was the fact that the village's usual schoolteacher, a brittle spinster whose scrawny neck made her look like a vulture, had fled south to avoid the advancing Germans.

Victor had a simple solution: Dominique, his wife, would

step into her shoes. Dominique, I suspected, had little say in the matter. As for me, the idea of sitting in a classroom with Philippe didn't exactly fill me with joy.

To make matters worse, the village was basking in the first real heat wave of the summer, but my father insisted on me going. What else was there to do anyway, except worry about when the Germans might show up? So I set off, a knot of apprehension in the pit of my stomach.

When I arrived at the classroom, I found to my surprise that it was deserted. I decided against hanging around on the off chance everyone would return, and wandered back toward the village, skirting the edge of the woods that led down to the river.

I hadn't gone far when I heard a scream, followed by another. I froze to the spot, straining to listen. It was Camille.

I broke into a run, cutting through the woods and tumbling down toward the river. Heart thumping, I leaped over fallen branches and swept through the undergrowth. This stretch was well upriver from the spot where we'd lost Christian's car, but as I careered down the hillside, I caught a glimpse of an old abandoned water mill just below, a huge wooden walkway jutting out above.

Finally I burst out of the woods and found myself standing on the riverbank.

To my astonishment, Camille, Philippe, the scruffy lad called Alphonse who'd crawled under everyone's legs at Victor's meeting and another younger boy I didn't know were swimming. Now they all turned to stare at me, equally astonished.

Camille, it suddenly became very clear, hadn't screamed because she was in trouble, but because the water was freezing.

A little farther away, on the same side of the river, Dominique was reclining on a towel, reading.

"Angelo . . . ," she said, a little flustered. She sat upright and quickly fastened a button on her blouse—her one concession to the hot weather. "I didn't realize you were starting today."

"Is school canceled?" I asked, trying to get my breath back.

"Not at all. We were just doing a little . . . botany fieldwork." I caught a familiar flicker of mischief in her eyes. I'd seen it once before, when she'd said how much she'd like to learn to drive.

"Come in!" Camille called over. My eyes darted to Philippe, who had clambered out onto the riverbank. He looked across at me, rather less welcoming.

I hesitated. "I'm not sure . . ."

"Why not?" Philippe called over. "Or isn't French water good enough for Italians?"

"Philippe!" Dominique scolded her son before turning to me. "Please, join us. You must be melting in this heat."

She was right. After my little sprint through the woods, I could feel a film of sweat soaking the back of my shirt—and the water did look so refreshing.

Without any further encouragement, I pulled off my shoes and shirt and rolled up my trousers. But nothing had prepared me for the shock of the icy water as I waded out into the river.

"Just dive under!" Camille shouted, seeing the blood

drain from my face. She grabbed her nose and plunged beneath the water, reappearing moments later, her long hair streaming with water. She flicked it behind her shoulders before turning to me, a look of malicious intent dancing in her eyes. I knew exactly what she was thinking.

"Oh no you d-don't . . . ," I stammered, backing away. By now the two younger boys were advancing on me in a pincer movement. As I glanced between them, I knew that my fate was sealed. Rather than fall into the hands of the enemy, I took the only honorable way out—and plunged into the freezing water.

As I burst back out, my head felt like it would split open from the stinging cold. But it didn't matter—it was exhilarating. Now that my toes weren't quite so numb, I could feel the smooth pebbles on the riverbed.

Philippe, who'd been watching from the side with a surly look on his face, called over to me again.

"If you're going to swim in our river, you have to pass our initiation test." His eyes darted up to the wooden beam jutting out above the abandoned water mill. "You have to dive off that."

"He will do no such thing," Dominique insisted. "And nor will you." She scowled at her son. "In fact, I think it's time we all headed back."

But Philippe didn't move. His eyes were drilling into me, daring me. "Unless, of course, you're too scared."

Until that moment my blood had felt frozen. Now I could feel it turning hot under his sneering gaze.

"I'll tell you what . . ." He smiled insolently. "I'll show you how it's done."

"Philippe, no . . . ," his mother protested. But he was already on his feet, scrabbling up the bank.

"He's only showing off," Camille tried to reassure me. "Don't give him the satisfaction."

"Have you done it?" I asked her.

"We all have," the youngest lad chimed in, smirking at me.

By now Philippe was clambering up the rotten timbers and edging out onto the beam above.

"Philippe, please," his mother called to him, but still he ignored her. From where I was standing shivering at the water's edge, the beam looked horribly high.

"Surely the water isn't deep enough?" I muttered.

"Best not to ask," Camille said. All at once I realized that if I didn't do this, I would be the only one. The only one and the Italian. Not only was I a traitor in Philippe's eyes; I would also be a coward. But as I squinted into the glare of the sun and saw him ready to leap, I knew I couldn't do it. The very thought made my stomach churn.

Philippe must have known, because he looked down at me smugly. Next thing I knew, he was running at full pelt. Beside me, Dominique clasped her hand to her mouth in fear; then Philippe was suddenly in midair. Muscular and sleek, he turned a full somersault before plunging headfirst into the water with barely a splash.

For several seconds there was no sign of him. Dominique took a step forward, beginning to panic, but a moment later he burst out of the water. With a few effortless strokes, he swam to the side and clambered out.

"Your turn," he said, getting his breath back.

I could feel my pulse racing. If I didn't do this, how would I hold my head up in front of Camille?

Fortunately the decision was taken out of my hands.

"As your teacher, I forbid you to do this."

I spun round to find Dominique fixing me with a steely look. Normally she was mild-mannered, almost submissive. But she was looking anything but submissive now.

"Everyone, back to class," she said firmly.

The others began silently tugging their clothes back on, avoiding eye contact with me. All except Philippe, who was staring at me, a sly smile of satisfaction on his face.

22 Undercover to Boutonne

"I know they're not what they were, but you should still try them."

It was a few hours after my humiliation by the river, and I was now sitting in Victor's bar, sulkily pushing one of Dominique's macaroons around my plate. Christian was still in Paris, so it was just my father and me at the table.

Since war had been declared, delicacies like chocolate and hazelnuts were rationed. Now they were almost impossible to come by, so Dominique had had to improvise, mainly by grinding up acorns from a nearby tree.

Living in the countryside, getting enough to eat wasn't as tough as it was in the cities. People simply grew their own. But clothes were harder to come by. I'd only just stopped wearing the flannel trousers my mother had forced me to wear when she'd first arrived in the village over a year and a half ago. As for the coveralls I'd ripped a hole in when I'd climbed into the old ambulance—that had long since been mended, though the patch had been joined by a colorful hotchpotch of others.

Seeing me brooding, my father clearly thought he knew what was getting me down.

"For all we know, the Germans have no idea we've been working on the car," he reassured me. "They're probably too busy trying to build their own. The Beetle, or whatever they're calling it. Apparently even Hitler is driving one as his staff car."

"Bertrand says they have their spies everywhere," I moaned. "And if they go to the factory, how long before they find out about the test track?"

The more I thought about it, the more inevitable it seemed that they would come looking in the village. And if they found we had been hiding the prototypes, who knew how they might punish us—not to mention the villagers.

My father sniffed dismissively, stealing my macaroon and planting it whole into his mouth. "If you ask me, you give those Germans far too much credit. Even if they do come, good luck to them. Because there's nothing to find."

I couldn't be sure if Papa was just saying this to put my mind at rest or because he really believed it. Either way, I didn't share his confidence.

Over the coming days and weeks, we carefully monitored the Germans' every move—as far as we were able, that is. Every evening we would gather round Victor's old Bakelite phone to speak to Bertrand. He was convinced that his phone calls, both at home and at work, were being listened in on by the Germans, so he went to huge lengths to call us from a different phone box each night. Sometimes it wasn't possible to place a call—the Germans had pulled down many of the telephone wires. But when we did speak to him, he kept us up-to-date on what was going on.

The Germans had arrived at the factory almost immediately after entering Paris and, as expected, announced that it was to be commandeered to make trucks for their own war effort.

No official mention was made of looking for the Tin Snail, but on the third day a different officer had arrived—someone called Major Tobias Keller, who began questioning Bertrand closely. Too closely. Over several days he interviewed every single worker in the factory—even Madame Detrice, Bertrand's long-suffering secretary.

"What exactly did he want to know?" my father asked anxiously as we huddled round to listen to Bertrand's call.

Bertrand's voice was thin and crackly at the other end.

"He never said anything specific. Just wanted to find out about all our recent projects. But he knows something, all right."

As I heard this, my heart clenched. Glancing nervously at my father and Victor, I could see that they were just as worried.

Whoever this Major Keller was, he was far too interested in everything Bertrand had been working on. But as Bertrand was only too pleased to point out, since a crater now stood where the offices had once been, all records of recent developments had been destroyed. There was no proof that we had been working on anything.

Eventually the German officer had left. It would now be a waiting game to see if he knew about the test track and turned up in the village, or whether we were safe.

Then, one evening, we got the news we had been dreading. Victor had spent the day in Boutonne on municipal business. When he stepped into the bar that evening, his best shirt was even more sweat-stained than usual. From the somber expression on his face it was clear that something was very wrong.

"What is it?" Dominique asked, fearing the worst.

"I've just come from the town hall," he announced. "They're expecting the Germans to arrive tonight."

As I heard his words, my heart turned to stone. If they were in Boutonne, only twenty kilometers away, surely they would come to Regnac? Possibly as soon as tomorrow.

This was it.

Victor immediately convened his war cabinet. In other words, a meeting that included my father, me, Félix, Benoît and whoever else was present in the bar at the time, presided over by himself, naturally.

"We don't know for sure they'll come to the village," Papa tried to reason.

"Our esteemed Italian friend is right." Victor nodded. "Boutonne is the seat of local government. It's only natural they would take over the town hall. They may just leave us alone."

Benoît's two teeth rattled against his pastis glass. "Oh, they'll come," he said. "If nothing else, they'll want to steal my wine."

"Then they'll take the horses," Félix grunted ominously.

"What should we do if they do come?" I asked warily.

"You must leave everything to me," Victor said. "As mayor, I will handle all official communications."

"I meant, what if they start searching?" I interrupted.

"Even if they do, we're prepared. Everything is buried. And what isn't, we have a perfectly innocent explanation for."

"We just have to hold our nerve and wait," my father urged. "The worst thing we can do now is start acting jumpy—then they'd be bound to get suspicious."

"I've got to go to the market in Boutonne tomorrow to sell some wine," Benoît croaked, nearly choking on a sip of pastis that had gone down the wrong way.

"Good." Victor nodded. "You can be our eyes and ears. See what's going on. But whatever you do, don't draw attention to yourself."

So it was agreed that Benoît would be our scout the following morning. He would report back if there was any sign the Germans were planning to take the bumpy little track toward Regnac.

When morning came, Benoît didn't look even remotely surprised to find me waiting for him as his horse-drawn cart rolled into the square.

"Hop on," he grunted, before coughing up a large gobbet of mucus and spitting into the dust.

"You knew I'd be here?" I asked, surprised, as I climbed on board.

"I figured as much," he said with a smirk. "Reckoned she would be here as well," he added, throwing a glance over my shoulder.

I spun round to find Camille heading over. "I—I don't understand," I stammered. "Are you going to market as well?"

"No," she answered matter-of-factly. "I'm going to spy on the Germans, just like you. Didn't think I'd let you have all the fun, did you?"

Nothing had prepared me for the sight of Boutonne when we finally arrived. The center of the town was overrun with German trucks, scout cars and motorbikes. For months, years even, I had been imagining what the enemy would look like. Now here they were in the flesh, crawling everywhere like ants. At every street corner huge rolls of barbed wire were being unfurled as road blocks and checkpoints were erected. The air was thick with the sound of hammering as sentry posts were constructed on every corner. New signposts in German gave directions for yet more army vehicles streaming into the central square.

I saw one of the soldiers hastily pasting a poster to the wall. It showed a smiling German storm trooper cradling a French child in his arms. All part of the Nazi Party's campaign to win over the locals.

Benoît gave me a nudge in the ribs as we trotted past. "Don't stare so hard," he growled under his breath.

I quickly looked the other way, just as a German guard began to take an interest in us.

"It's OK," Camille hissed a few moments later. "He's not looking anymore."

I allowed myself to breathe again. But if I was this terrified now, how would I cope if they came sniffing around the village?

When we reached the covered market, there was a sense

of real panic in the air. Those who had ventured out were buying up meat as quickly as they could, loading everything they could manage onto carts and bicycles. Who knew how long before supplies ran out?

"Maybe this wasn't such a good idea after all," Benoît whispered, carefully watching a pair of German soldiers who were starting to check people's papers. "We should go."

"But we've only just got here," Camille protested.

"Let's just say I don't fancy explaining to that lot what I've got under my blanket."

I lifted a corner and peered underneath. There were several flagons of special home brew nestled under some straw. Benoît's hand snatched the blanket from me and replaced it carefully.

"You trying to get us arrested?" he snapped. His roguish charm had vanished. Instead, for the first time, I saw that he was scared. Having lived through one war, he had a much better idea of what to expect.

He geed the horse on and we trotted away from the market before the German soldiers could reach us.

Before long we were back at the turnoff for Regnac, just in time to see a troop of soldiers spill out of the back of a truck to erect a checkpoint. As we continued on our journey home, none of us spoke. Our mission may have ended much more abruptly than we'd expected, but I was relieved just to make it out.

When I thought it was safe, I finally glanced back over my shoulder, half expecting to see the soldiers coming after us. They weren't—for the moment, at least.

That night I hardly slept at all. I kept imagining I could

hear the distant rumble of enemy tanks rolling across the fields, flattening everything before them.

When I ventured into the square the following morning, I fully expected to find it surrounded by barbed wire, with a sentry demanding to see my papers. But it was all as sleepy as usual. Hard to believe the might of the German army was so close. Yet as the day wore on, and then the next, still there was no distant rumble of caterpillar tracks descending on the village.

The following day I went back to school. I had to do something, or the suspense of waiting for the Germans to arrive would drive me crazy. But by late morning Dominique announced it was time for another botany field trip—which was now official code for messing about by the river.

Fortunately Philippe was helping out his father with council business: Victor was arranging for him to do an apprenticeship of sorts in the planning department down in Boutonne. But first he would have to sit some exams. It was the very last thing Philippe wanted to do, but since France was no longer at war, there was little choice.

As the days began to merge into each other, our botany field trips to the river became increasingly frequent. For those brief hours spent playing in the water, all thought of the impending invasion slowly slipped from our minds. It was like the war was something that was happening everywhere else, and so long as we remained by the river, it would always stay like that.

After our daily swim, once our clothes had dried, I would walk back into the village with Camille. At the fork in the road, the left track led down the hill and then steeply up to the manor house, beside the avenue of cypresses where the cows liked to graze in the shade. The right track led to the village and Camille's house.

One afternoon, I noticed that Camille seemed particularly distracted. As we came to the fork, she paused. I had already walked on several meters before I realized she had stopped.

"What?" I asked.

"I just assumed you'd be heading home," she answered, trying to appear casual.

"Why?"

"No reason." She shrugged and carried on walking. But as we continued toward the village, my mind started to turn over her remark. What would make her stop like that?

My question would soon get an answer. As we approached the square, Camille became more and more withdrawn. I glanced at her and saw, possibly for the first time ever, that her face had colored.

"What's wrong?"

"What makes you think anything's wrong?" she answered shortly. But it was clear from her tone that something was up. "I have to go," she muttered, before heading quickly across the square.

As I watched her, my heart suddenly lurched—for this time she didn't carry on to the forge, but went into the café. Where Philippe was waiting for her.

How could this be? Surely Camille couldn't like him. As if to add insult to injury, Camille didn't look back once as she hurried away. But Philippe did. He turned and stared at me—a lingering, malevolent look.

I turned and headed home, feeling physically sick.

That night I barely touched my food—what there was of it. My father was too distracted to notice as he listened, absorbed, to the news on the radio about the German advance toward Bordeaux. So I went off to bed early and lay awake on top of my covers, fully dressed.

After what must have been several hours, I woke and sat bolt upright in bed. I was still fully dressed and sweating. The curtains were rustling in a breeze that made the window frame tap against the shutters. Something in the air had changed. The wind had altered direction, and now blew hot and dusty from the south, straight from Africa.

I couldn't face trying to go back to sleep. Instead, I slipped silently out of my room and down the stone stairs, eased the front door open and crept out into the courtyard.

Ten minutes later I had wandered into the village square, now eerily silent. I sat on a bench and tried to clear my head, but it was no use. No matter how hard I tried to block it out, all I could think of was Camille and Philippe.

Suddenly something hit the ground next to me—perhaps an acorn dislodged by a bird or a squirrel. I had just decided to ignore it when a stone landed right beside my foot. I spun round to find Camille standing on the other side of the scruffy patch where the locals played boules.

"Couldn't sleep?"

I shrugged. "Too hot."

She sat next to me on the bench and I felt the warm down on her arm brush lightly against my skin.

"I know you're angry with me," she said after a moment.

"Why would I be angry?" I asked, trying to hide the sarcasm in my voice and failing.

"Because of Philippe." She sighed.

"Can you blame me?"

"Actually, I think it's rather sweet."

"Sweet?" I asked, indignant.

"Admit it," she said. "You're jealous."

I couldn't believe what I was hearing, partly because it was so true. I had a mind to tell her right then and there what he'd said about her mother and father. But even now I couldn't bring myself to repeat his vile words.

"For goodness' sake," she groaned, rolling her eyes. "I'm only teasing you. He isn't my boyfriend."

"Oh," I said, completely wrong-footed.

"Give me some credit. I just promised to help him with some of his exam stuff."

I felt like a prize idiot. For a moment we sat in silence. Then, before I knew what I was doing, I was suddenly up on my feet.

"Come on."

"Where are you going?" she asked, confused.

But by now I was already halfway across the square.

By the time she caught up with me, I was racing toward the woods. Moments later we arrived at the riverbank. The old water mill and the wooden beam loomed above us in the darkness.

"You want to go swimming now?" she asked in disbelief.

"Not quite," I corrected her.

At that, her eyes followed mine up to the beam. Suddenly she understood. "Maybe this isn't such a good idea. . . ." She faltered.

"If I don't do it now, I never will," I told her, feeling my heart start to race even faster.

Before I could talk myself out of it, I began climbing up the rotten woodwork of the water mill. Before long I was taking my first tentative step out onto the beam.

If I thought it was high when I was down below, it was nothing compared to what it looked like now. My stomach knotted sickeningly as I peered down at the inky black water far below. I was beginning to think that maybe this wasn't such a good idea after all when Camille shinned up the woodwork and appeared next to me.

"So you're really going to do it?" she asked, intrigued.

"You've done it, haven't you?" But for a moment I thought I saw a flicker of hesitation in her eye.

"Of course I have," she scoffed and, as if to prove her point, nudged past me, edging her way out toward the end of the beam.

I felt my stomach clench again. "M-maybe you should come back," I stammered.

"Quickest way to go down is to jump," she said, smiling mischievously.

She took a step backward along the beam and I felt my heart leap into my mouth.

"Don't be stupid. . . ."

"So stop me," she goaded, before taking another step toward the edge.

I couldn't believe she was putting me in this situation. That I'd put myself in this situation.

Then, all at once, I was running. I don't remember giving

my legs permission to do it, yet here they were, apparently taking on a life of their own. What's more, my throat had joined in and was now letting out a banshee wail of terror. Camille screamed as I suddenly leaped toward her, sending us both somersaulting backward over the edge.

For what seemed like an eternity our bodies twisted through the darkness, until we finally crashed into the icy water below. When we eventually resurfaced, we swam back to the bank, and sprawled on our backs, trying to get our breath back.

"What the . . . ?" Camille spluttered, staring at me, wild-eyed.

"What?" I protested. "You told me to do it."

"I wasn't serious! Jesus, you could have killed me!"

"Hold on. You haven't dived in from there before, have you?" I asked, outraged.

"Of course not!" she snapped. "Do you think I'm stupid?"

I stared at her for a second, then burst out laughing, partly out of relief that I was still alive, partly because I had proved myself to her.

Then, just as suddenly, I stopped. Far off, I heard a rumbling that seemed to make the very earth shudder.

We turned and looked at each other. We both knew without saying exactly what it was.

The Germans.

23 The Germans Arrive

By the time we made it back to the village, a large Panzer tank had taken up residence in the center of the square. In negotiating the corner, one of its enormous caterpillar tracks had mounted the curb and crushed the stonework into rubble. Beside the tank was a German scout car and several motorbikes with sidecars. About twenty German soldiers were milling around, eyeing the windows for any sign of hostility.

Victor suddenly emerged, hastily tugging on his mono-grammed dressing gown and trying to muster as much authority as he could, while several other locals wandered out cautiously. Amid the deafening noise of the tank and motorbikes, Victor began to remonstrate with one of the German soldiers, demanding to know who was in charge.

Suddenly a large military staff car thundered into the square. Its huge radiator grille and sweeping wheel arches were caked in dust, but I recognized it immediately: a Mercedes Benz 770—the most expensive and luxurious car the German manufacturer made. Adolf Hitler himself drove one.

As it drew to a halt, one of the soldiers leaped forward to open the rear door and an imperious-looking German officer stepped out. Around his neck hung a silver insignia on a chain. It glinted in the moonlight, and I saw the sinister skull and crossbones of the Panzer division.

The officer calmly removed his goggles and elbow-length gloves and glanced around. He was extremely compact and neat, his uniform immaculately starched. His nose was razor sharp and tilted upwards. I could see his nostrils sniff the air, almost as if he were trying to pick up a scent, while his small, narrow eyes darted cunningly around the square.

He nodded respectfully to some of the locals before his hawk-like eyes picked out Victor. As he made his way over, Victor drew himself up to his full height and pulled in his stomach importantly.

"Are you in charge?" Victor barked.

The officer gave a broad smile. It was obviously supposed to convey warmth, and yet somehow it seemed too practiced, too mechanical.

"I am Major Tobias Keller," he said, extending a hand courteously to Victor.

My blood ran cold at the sound of his name. This was the very man Bertrand had told us about. The officer who had interrogated all the workers at the factory.

They must have found out about the test track—or

known about it all along. And now they were here, looking for our car. Thank goodness we had destroyed everything, I reassured myself.

But then a terrible thought dawned on me. Already there were rumors of the Nazi secret police taking people away to interrogate them in towns and cities all over the country. What if they arrested my father and tortured him . . . ?

I began scratching nervously at the back of my neck, then put my hand down by my side for fear of giving myself away.

Victor, meanwhile, made no attempt to shake the major's extended hand, so he calmly withdrew it.

"May I assume that you are the mayor here?" Keller asked, in crisp, educated French.

"I am," Victor informed him coldly.

"Then we are to become acquainted. As you are no doubt aware, under the agreements of the armistice, you are under the jurisdiction of the Wehrmacht. However, so long as you offer no resistance, I am more than happy for you to carry out your duties as usual. It is my sincere hope that we can work together to our"—the major paused to find the right word—"mutual benefit."

Victor was a little thrown. I think he expected to have to make a stand, but the German officer had taken the wind out of his sails by saying that nothing would change. How were you supposed to defy that?

"I see . . ." He faltered. But feeling the eyes of the villagers on him, he clearly felt he had to put up some show of defiance.

"Your tank has destroyed the curbstone," he grumbled, indicating where the tracks had mounted the pavement.

The major immediately unleashed a barrage of furious orders to the tank commander. Suddenly a huge plume of black fumes belched out of the vehicle's funnel as it rumbled backward, exposing more destroyed stonework.

Keller turned to Victor. "My apologies. My men will have it repaired first thing in the morning."

Again Victor was disarmed by his respectful tone.

"Now, may I impose on you for a suggestion as to where I may billet my men?" the major asked courteously. "I will also require rooms for myself and my guest."

Guest? I glanced back at the staff car and saw that there was a second occupant—a small, mousy-looking civilian buried under a large coat and hat and clutching a case. I couldn't place him, but something about him seemed strangely familiar. We had met somewhere before.

At that moment my father raced up to join me.

"Are you OK?" he asked breathlessly. I nodded—but his attention had already been drawn to the small figure hunched in the back of the Mercedes. I saw from his look that he had recognized him immediately.

"What is it?" I demanded.

"The man in the back," Papa muttered darkly. "He was at the motor show. He's Ferdinand Porsche's right-hand man."

I looked again. Sure enough, it was the same weaselly fellow I had seen bustling around at the motor show all that time ago.

It was odd. For so long we had talked of our German rivals coming to the village with their spies, yet now that one was right here in front of us, he looked entirely harmless. Almost disappointing.

However, the news that the Germans intended to stay in the village sent a shiver down my spine. They must know.

"May I ask why you feel it necessary to occupy a village as small as this?" Victor asked the German major curtly.

My father tensed. If Victor appeared too concerned about the Germans staying, it might arouse suspicion.

"We have some business in this area," Major Keller replied crisply. "Unrelated to the war."

"May I ask what?"

Now even I knew that Victor was in danger of pushing too far.

"It's a private matter. Nothing that need concern you," the major assured him. His tone was slightly less cordial this time.

Victor caught Papa's eye—a worried glance that was met by a steely look from my father and the very subtlest of head shakes. He was obviously telling Victor not to push the matter. Victor turned away, but it was too late. Keller had picked up on the glance and was now looking over at us.

My guts tensed as I waited to see what would happen. It was hard to say whether Keller had recognized my father. After a moment his piercing eyes turned back to Victor.

"So, the rooms?"

"We have one or two above the bar," Victor grunted. "Otherwise the nearest hotel is twenty kilometers away in Boutonne. You may prefer to stay there."

"No problem." Keller smiled. "I saw a large manor house as we turned off the road. It will more than suffice for me and my men."

My stomach clenched again. Were they really going to take over Bertrand's house? What would become of us?

My father stepped out of the shadows and cleared his throat. "Excuse me."

Major Keller turned slowly, and I suddenly saw how steely his eyes looked in the moonlight.

"The house you mentioned is already occupied. By me and my son," Papa stated coolly.

The German officer calmly weighed him up before smiling. "Then we are to be your guests," he said. "The house looked more than big enough from what I could see from the road."

Before my father could protest, Keller was rattling out orders to his men. Anything Papa tried to say was immediately drowned out by the roar of engines starting up.

For all the officer's politeness, I realized that resistance was not an option. As of now, the German army, and the spy from Porsche's company, were not just in the village; they were in Bertrand's house.

As the vehicles started to maneuver their way out of the square in a huge roar of activity, my attention flitted back to the hunched little man in the Mercedes. He was watching my father with beady little eyes. There could be no doubt now: he knew who my father was. But for the moment he said nothing.

The German soldiers were billeted in various barns and outbuildings of the manor house, their assortment of vehicles neatly parked around the courtyard. Of course, the tank was too large to fit through the gates, so it squatted in the adjoining field with Benoît's bull to keep it company.

Keller himself took over one of the rooms on the ground floor, sleeping in a camp bed next door to the makeshift office we had set up in the breakfast room. It unnerved me to think that, until recently, those very walls had been covered in sketches and diagrams for the Tin Snail.

Porsche's spy, meanwhile, had disappeared into a small room toward the back of the house. As soon as he arrived, my father studiously avoided making eye contact with him, but I knew it would be impossible to avoid him for long.

That night was the longest of my life. To think that for the last week or so I'd allowed myself to imagine that the Germans might not come after all; now here they were, sleeping under the very same roof as us.

More to the point, how long would it be before my father, or even I, became Major Keller's next interrogation victim?

24 Pains au Chocolat!

I woke early, and did what I always do when my nerves get the better of me: I tried to keep busy. It wasn't long before my curiosity about the tank became overwhelming and, while the soldiers were shaving and washing in various corners of the courtyard, I wandered over for a closer look.

It was a terrifying piece of engineering, ruthlessly efficient and bristling with power. I shrank at the thought of the villages it had crushed beneath its vast tracks as it rumbled its way south.

"Step up and look inside," a voice suddenly called from behind me. I spun round to find Major Keller smiling benignly. He was less formal now, without his double-breasted overcoat. Instead he wore only striped black jodhpurs and a shirt. But he was still, I noticed, immaculately presented, his sharp chin closely shaved, and his boots gleaming.

I hesitated. I wanted to look inside so badly, but I felt it was wrong, like a betrayal.

"I'd rather not," I mumbled. "But thank you anyway."

Keller raised an eyebrow, surprised. "Perhaps another time. We should be here for quite a while."

I smiled awkwardly and made to head back inside.

"Your name . . . ," the major continued, curious. "Angelo. That's Italian, of course. Your father named you, perhaps, after the great artist, Michelangelo?"

My heart started to thump harder.

"I need to go," I muttered, then turned and headed back across the gravel. I wanted to run, but I knew I must stay calm. With every step, I felt the major's eyes boring into the back of my neck, to that raw patch of skin where my collar always rubbed.

When I reached the back door, my father was waiting for me on the pantry steps.

"What did he ask you?"

"Nothing," I whispered furtively. "He just wanted to know if my name was Italian."

My father sighed and I looked at him, heavyhearted.

"He knows, doesn't he?"

"He certainly knows something, otherwise he wouldn't be here. But that doesn't mean he's going to find anything," he reassured me. "Come on."

"Where are we going?"

"Into town. I need to talk to Victor."

But as we turned the corner of the house to head toward the gates, our way was blocked by a German soldier, a rifle slung over his arm.

"The major has asked that you are kindly joining him for breakfast," he barked in broken French.

"We're eating in the village. But thank him anyway." My father made to skirt the soldier, but he stepped in front of us, barring our exit.

"It was not a question."

A few moments later we were ushered into the breakfast room. Major Keller was pulling on his jacket when we entered, and he looked up, all smiles.

My eyes nearly burst out of their sockets when I saw what was on the table. It was covered in a huge spread of delicacies, the likes of which I had barely seen before, especially not since the austere rationing had kicked in. My father had also spotted them, and swallowed hard. Every kind of chocolate pastry and sticky tartlet was here.

Could the major somehow have known about my father's sweet tooth? The idea was absurd, and yet . . .

"Ah, I'm so glad you could join me." Keller beamed. "Please, sit. We have brought some extra rations, as you can see."

"I don't feel comfortable eating this while the rest of the country are eating acorns," my father responded tersely.

"You need have no worry on that front. My men will start distributing extra rations this morning," Keller told him. "So we all have reason to celebrate the ending of hostilities." He turned to me, picking up a pain au chocolat. "They're not as good as Parisian ones, but the chocolate inside is first-rate.

Try some." He thrust it toward me. I took it reluctantly, eyeing my father uncertainly.

"Please," the major continued, "do me the courtesy of joining me for a few moments. We have much to discuss."

At that moment the door opened and the mousy figure of Keller's companion appeared. He glanced up, blinking like a mole in the sunshine streaming in through the French windows.

"Herr Engel, perfect timing," Keller greeted him, then turned to my father. "I believe you may know each other already?"

My heart clenched tighter.

"Of course," my father said, nodding slightly. The German engineer smiled back nervously and fumbled to free his hand from his briefcase.

"Mr. Fabrizzi. We met at the Paris Motor Show. May I say how much I admired your aerodynamic design," Engel said. "Quite extraordinary. I was sorry that it did not get the admiration it deserved. And that it met with that little accident . . . ," he added awkwardly.

"Well," said my father, "the 'little accident,' as you call it, was nothing compared to the setback it suffered when your army invaded our country."

"Strictly speaking, that would be Major Keller's army," Engel corrected, casting an awkward glance at Keller.

"Quite right!" Major Keller was clearly eager to lighten the mood. "Now please, eat."

With that, he began to stuff his face with one of the pains au chocolat, swooning with theatrical delight.

"These are unbelievable, *ja?*"

I discreetly tore a piece off the end of mine and slipped it into my mouth. After so long without, the chocolate tasted exquisitely sweet as it oozed down my throat.

Keller gesticulated at me excitedly. "Put some of the chocolate in your milk. Trust me, it's truly sinful." His eyes sparkled with pleasure.

As he rammed still more of the pastry into his mouth, I watched Engel more closely. His hands were delicate, like hamster paws, as they carefully removed his spectacles and placed them on the table. I could see that he was fastidious, a man of detail and precision, but also of infinite gentleness as he spread out his napkin in his lap. He suddenly caught me watching him and smiled bashfully, his eyes surprisingly kind.

I glanced at my father, who was carefully stirring his thick black coffee. I recognized the telltale signs: his mind was calculating as he began spooning in more and more sugar.

Keller had obviously noticed too. "Ah, you have a sweet tooth as well, I see."

My father stopped and carefully laid the spoon down on the saucer. Some of the coffee had spilled over the top, just as it always did, staining the tablecloth.

By now Engel was staring awkwardly at his spartan breakfast of a fig and some heavy black German bread. It seemed he didn't share our sweet tooth.

Funny, I thought. If he wasn't the enemy, I could almost imagine him and Bertrand getting along.

"What is it you want from us?" my father asked eventually, looking the major squarely in the eye.

"Straight to the point. Good, I like directness," Keller said approvingly. "My friend Herr Engel here is a huge fan of your work. In fact, he has talked of very little else since we left Paris. . . ." He stopped and looked uncertain. "Did I mention that we had spoken with your Monsieur Hipaux? A most fascinating man."

My father did his best not to reveal that he knew this already.

"How is Bertrand?"

Keller grinned slyly. "Very obliging. We've asked him to tweak some of his plans to help with our war effort."

"Tweak?" Papa asked. He obviously liked the sound of it even less than I did.

Keller was quick to reassure us. "Just to concentrate on vehicles—trucks mainly—for military use."

"I'm surprised he can make anything," my father snapped. "Seeing as you bombed most of the factory."

"That was very regrettable," Keller sighed, tearing off another piece of pastry and cramming it into his mouth. "Nonetheless, I think it will be a very fruitful relationship.

"One thing intrigues me," he continued, still chewing. "I asked Herr Engel here to take a look over the books—to see what the company has been developing over the last year. Shall I tell you what I found? Nothing. Isn't that strange?"

I felt my insides turn to water. Keller was onto us; there could be no doubt about it. I hardly dared look at my father. But when I did, he appeared calm and unruffled.

"As you know"—he smiled coolly—"our latest designs met with a 'little accident' when you dropped that bomb on the factory. Besides," he went on, "what would be the point of designing a new car when we were at war? Where would be the sense in that?"

I stole a furtive look at Engel to see if he was buying it. If he was suspicious, his face gave little away as he chewed neatly on his fig.

Major Keller studied my father closely. "Perhaps. Or perhaps you have been developing a vehicle you didn't want the world to know about. One you wanted to keep all to yourselves." He smiled wolfishly.

I closed my eyes, sensing the inevitable, but my father held his nerve.

"Then it was so secret, even I was not informed. Although that would hardly surprise me."

Engel looked up, suddenly puzzled. "Why would you say that?"

Papa turned to him. "Herr Engel, you of all people must have heard the rumors?"

"What rumors?" Keller interjected, his curiosity getting the better of him now.

"It was explained to me that my services as a designer were, shall we say, surplus to requirements. Why else do you think we would move here of all places?" my father said. "Bertrand is too good a man to leave me to starve, so he said I could become caretaker of this house."

Engel lowered his fig to his plate. "If this is true, then I am sorry. I happen to believe that your work is some of the best I have ever seen."

"Thank you," my father replied sincerely. "Unfortunately our shareholders did not share your good opinion."

I breathed more freely again. Papa had been clever, his lies so close to the truth that it would be hard to see where the truth ended and the lie began.

But if Engel was taken in, Major Keller was less easily duped.

"Well, this is all most perplexing," he declared, wiping his mouth vigorously before throwing his napkin down on the table.

"Why?" my father asked, feigning innocence.

"Because we had it on the greatest authority that you have been developing a car, right here, in this village. The Führer himself has expressed an interest in seeing it."

It was all I could do not to spray my hot chocolate across the table in a gasp of amazement. Hitler himself wanted to see our car?

Keller shot a look at me. "Did something I say surprise you?" he asked, arching an eyebrow.

"The—the drink," I stammered. "It was hot."

My father glared reproachfully at me before turning back to Keller. "What on earth would give you that idea?"

"Come, come, Signor Fabrizzi, let us not play games. . . . Did you really think I didn't know about your little test track here?"

"If there is one, it was long before my time," my father replied dismissively. "Can I also ask why the leader of the Third Reich would be interested in a piffling French car design anyway?"

The major turned to his companion. "Herr Engel, perhaps you should explain. . . ."

Engel fingered his glasses nervously. "For some time now, my team have been working on what we call a 'people's car.' It is something very close to the Führer's heart. But we were reliably informed by a"—he hesitated before carrying on—"source that you too have been developing just such a vehicle. Naturally, given your reputation for innovation, we would be most interested to—"

"Steal it?" The words leaped out of my mouth before I could stop them. I smiled as Keller eyed me suspiciously.

"I was going to say collaborate"—Engel paused for a minute—"on a joint venture. After all, our two companies share a lot of similar goals."

"You'll have to excuse me," Papa interrupted, "but it was German designers who gave us that brutish monstrosity parked outside." He was referring, of course, to the tank. "And now you've turned our factory in Paris into a production line for personnel carriers. I don't see how we can share many values at all." He'd abandoned any pretense of indifference now: his blood was well and truly up.

Keller drummed his fingers on the table, thoughtful. "In that case we shall have to put our little collaboration on the people's car to one side. In the meantime, I would be most grateful, Signor Fabrizzi—"

"Monsieur Fabrizzi," my father corrected him. "I think of myself as French now."

"Ah, of course . . . ," the major responded. "Nonetheless, I would be grateful to you if you could guide me around your new home away from home."

"Forgive me, but the locals hold me in enough suspicion as it is, without seeing me as a traitor."

"Very well." Keller sighed. "Then perhaps Angelo won't mind."

I opened my mouth to protest, but he was already on his feet.

"Good, that's settled."

25 The Beer Pump

I reluctantly followed one of Major Keller's men out into the courtyard to find the Mercedes purring, the driver standing stiffly at attention beside it.

At first Keller was nowhere to be seen. Then, with a rush of panic, I saw him. He was standing by the open door to the old garage. I urged myself to keep calm. After all, what was there to be found? Just the dusty old remains of the ambulance. I shuffled closer, trying not to betray my nerves. Keller, now resplendent in his finest cavalry outfit, was studying the ambulance curiously.

"Such a shame," he murmured as I drew closer. "An old relic like this should be in a museum. But I suppose it's little wonder it's fallen apart. After all, it was made in France."

"Actually, it was a Rolls-Royce," I said, surprising myself with my nerve.

"Even more fitting that it's just junk now," he sneered. "But enough idle banter. We have a guided tour to begin." He strode off across the gravel to his waiting car.

For a moment I lingered behind him, studying the ambulance. It was strange. I'd remembered my father and Christian stripping down loads of parts to use in the first prototypes—so how come they hadn't been buried with everything else? I decided that my father, like Keller, assumed they were too old and useless to be suspicious.

I hurried back to join the major. The driver held open the car door for his commanding officer, but instead Keller turned to me.

"After you," he said with a smile.

I glanced at the driver, who looked faintly affronted at having to hold the door for a scruffy teenager. I clambered in and was joined by Keller, who thumped down into the leather upholstery next to me.

"Where shall we go first?" he asked, his voice heavy with irony. "I think maybe the bar tabac. I always find that's a good source of local information."

The huge engine roared into life and the car surged forward, crunching on the gravel as it swept through the gates and turned right toward the village.

Keller surveyed the countryside as the car roared along, passing cows that lifted their heads lazily to see what the noise was about.

"You know, I grew up in a village much like this one," he

shouted over the sound of the rushing wind. I thought he almost looked wistful. Then we thundered past a trough of silage by the side of the road and his face fell. "I hated every minute of it."

When we swung left into the village, I looked around the square with alarm. Several large personnel trucks had pulled in and were now spewing out troops.

"I've changed my mind," the major suddenly announced. "I think before we visit the bar I should like to see Bertrand's old test track. You can show me, *ja?*"

My face went white and I thought I might actually be sick. What if there were still some traces of the work we had done there?

"Well?" Keller smiled at me, waiting for an answer.

I cleared my throat. "I—I don't know anything about a test track," I stammered.

He fixed me with a terrifying stare. "Surely a car enthusiast like your father talked to you about Bertrand's famous test track."

I could see there was no way out of it. He only had to ask someone in the village and he would find it.

"My father did once mention an old field where Bertrand tried out his first cars, if that's what you mean," I muttered. "I think it's that way." I indicated the road leading out of town.

Keller shouted harshly to the driver and the car leaped forward again.

Ten minutes later we swept into the field that until so recently had been the Tin Snail's unofficial test track. In the ten months since the order had been given to destroy every last trace of the prototypes, the grass had grown high again, all but concealing the original cracked tarmac.

Keller threw open his door and leaped out. He walked forward and surveyed the field while I waited sheepishly by the car.

The field looked exactly like a field. Keller's eyes narrowed as he studied it shrewdly. His face was very still as he sniffed the air; then he bent down to examine the earth, pulling away a little clump of weeds to reveal tire tracks.

"I see that someone has been driving a lot of vehicles through here. A year ago, maybe less."

"Benoît's barn is down there," I offered by way of explanation, pointing to beyond the wooded copse.

"These are not the tracks of a tractor," Keller persisted. "At least, not all of them." He looked up at me from under the shadow of his peaked cap and I could see his black eyes drilling into me, searching for the truth.

After a moment his expression softened again. He looked behind me, at the large corrugated-iron shed that had so recently been our workshop.

"And what might this be?" he asked brightly, striding toward it in his well-polished cavalry boots.

The doors were locked. With a nod from Keller, the driver smashed the lock off with the butt of his rifle. The major pulled the doors wide-open, and sunshine poured into the cavernous recesses of the workshop.

To my relief, it was completely empty—not a single rivet or bolt had been left.

Keller paced around it, clearly curious. "It's strange, is it not—a place like this, left completely empty . . ."

It was a good point. Benoît should at least have hauled a few rusty old bits of farm machinery in to make it looked used.

"No matter." Keller shrugged, turning on his heels and striding back to the staff car. He paused briefly, seeing I hadn't followed him.

"I should really be going to school," I told him, and he grinned again.

"Today school is canceled. You know what? I think we will take a trip to that bar now."

As before, it was not so much an invitation as an order.

Engel was sitting waiting for us. He stood up awkwardly as we approached, nodding to the major before giving me a ghost of a nervous smile. Victor bustled over, looking anxious when he saw me with them.

"We'd like the menu, if you please," Keller announced.

"Of course." Victor nodded. "And to drink?"

Keller jerked his head toward me. "I imagine my young friend here would appreciate another hot chocolate."

I tried to protest, but Keller dismissed it.

"Nonsense. Victor's wife received a new batch of chocolate only this morning, courtesy of the Wehrmacht." Then he turned to Engel. "Perhaps you will join me in a local beer, Herr Engel?"

But Engel shook his head. "As you know, Major, I never drink in the morning. Just a small black tea, please."

Victor nodded and headed away.

"So, Angelo," Keller continued, eyeing me. "Is it really true that your father hasn't been working on a new car?"

I went rigid with tension, and even Engel dabbed nervously at his forehead.

The major patted me on the shoulder. "Don't worry, my little Michelangelo. Even if you don't tell us, we'll find out. It will be an enjoyable game."

I looked away, catching Engel's eye briefly. The German designer sat squirming in his seat, evidently not enjoying this "game" much either.

Suddenly I spotted something and froze on the spot. Over Engel's shoulder, Dominique was drawing a large glass of beer from the pump—which, with a start, I recognized. It was the gearstick from one of the prototypes!

I was terrified—and yet also just a little bit exhilarated. Here was a senior officer in the German army, about to enjoy a beer pulled by a gearstick from the very car he and his men were searching for.

When Victor brought over Keller's beer, it was all I could do to stop myself smirking. And yet . . . if Keller turned and saw the beer pump, surely the game was up?

The major cast a long, calculating look around the room. "Tell me. The implements above the bar . . ."

I glanced nervously up at the wall. Various old farming tools had been mounted for decoration.

"What about them?" Victor asked evenly.

"They are for plowing, am I right?"

"They were here when I bought the place," he replied dismissively.

But Keller was already out of his seat, striding across the

room to the bar, where Dominique was serving. "May I see one?"

Dominique flicked a wary glance to her husband, and I suddenly realized that something was wrong. Engel had noticed it too. His gerbil eyes narrowed as he watched them closely.

Victor calmly approached the bar and reached up to unhook the large plowing yoke. Now I too saw the danger: next to it was a piece of equipment rather different in origin—and rather more recent. It was a piece of the crankshaft from the Tin Snail, and beside it was the rudimentary starting handle for the engine.

I held my breath as Victor passed the yoke to the major, who examined it, apparently fascinated.

"Remarkable. If I'm not mistaken, this is at least a hundred years old." He handed the wooden implement back. "And yet . . . the pieces next to it"—he craned his neck to peer at the wall—"seem altogether more modern."

If Victor was alarmed, he masked it perfectly. He leaned toward the officer and murmured conspiratorially, "Actually, they fell off old Benoît's tractor. I thought they might look the part for any passing tourists."

Keller stared at him, before a smile spread slowly across his face. "Well, I'm afraid this particular tourist has not fallen for your little trick. But don't worry," he said, pressing a finger to his lips for comical effect, "your secret is safe with me." With that, he sauntered back to join us at the table.

I watched Dominique out of the corner of my eye. As he passed, Victor gently stroked her arm for reassurance.

When I looked back, Keller was watching me searchingly.

"Well, Angelo, I think it is time you and I had a full and frank discussion." He wiped some beer froth from his top lip before continuing. "I can't help feeling that you're holding something back from me. If you told me everything now, you could save everyone—especially your father—a lot of unnecessary suffering."

I felt my stomach cramp. Just how long would I be able to keep up the pretense of knowing nothing?

"Major Keller?" Engel interjected. "Perhaps the boy actually does know nothing. Would we not be better off concentrating on talking to the adults?"

Keller considered the matter for a moment. "Perhaps you're right," he conceded. "Yes, in fact, I think the time has come to expand our little list of interviewees. We shall start interrogating everyone in the village—with immediate effect."

As his ominous words hung in the air, he raised his glass to both of us, then downed his beer quickly. A dribble trickled down the side of his mouth and dripped onto the butt of his pistol, just visible, gleaming inside its holster.

26 Hide-and-Seek

Over the coming days Major Keller's men systematically searched every living room, outhouse, barn, workshop and shed in the entire village. No pillow, turnip patch, wine barrel or liquor still was left unturned. But they found nothing.

During this search, the soldiers, following Keller's express instructions, took meticulous care not to make a mess. At one point, one overzealous storm trooper knocked a jug to the floor in Marguerite's kitchen. She scolded the clumsy culprit, even threatening to beat him with a spoon. The hapless soldier, barely out of his teens, was humiliated by this tirade and things could easily have turned ugly. But Keller was quick to step in and tear a strip off the beleaguered soldier, who was then forced to scrub Marguerite's floor for three hours by way of punishment. After that there were no more breakages.

Two more days of searching passed, each as fruitless as the one before. Until, on the third, Keller and his men were passing the cemetery behind the church. Camille and I had been shadowing their movements most of the day, anxious to keep an eye on where they were searching while trying to appear as inconspicuous as we could. But as the Germans filed past the graveyard, Keller turned unexpectedly. His gimlet eyes surveyed it and suddenly found Camille, who was pretending to leave a few daffodils by a grave. I was standing next to her, desperately trying to look natural.

"What's he doing?" Camille hissed as I glanced at my upside-down school book.

"Walking over here," I hissed back. "Stop shaking."

"I'm not!" she muttered crossly, but her hands rattled the jam jar she was filling with flowers.

Suddenly Keller was looming over us. "How nice to see young people showing such respect to the dead," he purred. Suddenly one of the graves caught his attention. "This is most unusual," he mused, studying the lie of the land. "The grass on this grave is much greener. Now, why would that be?"

Of course, Camille and I knew exactly why: because, only a matter of months ago, we had excavated the grave and buried, amongst other things, a gearbox and carburetor there. When we had filled the hole in again, Marguerite had thrown in some of her prize pig fertilizer to help the grass regrow. Which was exactly what it had done—only far too well, it seemed.

I felt my legs begin to buckle. Keller turned to his men and shouted something in German; it sounded like machine-gun fire. Before Camille and I knew what was happening, the men were crawling over the cemetery with pickaxes and spades.

Seconds later, the first blade sank into the soft earth of the burial mound.

Camille and I hardly dared look at each other. It was surely only a matter of time before Keller dug up the coffin and discovered exactly what lay underneath.

After exactly twenty-three minutes, a dull thud emanated from the hole the soldiers had now dug. It was the sound of a spade hitting wood. Spotting the commotion, several of the villagers had rushed over to protest. Keller refused to listen to them, driving his men on to dig deeper. Now, as Victor himself approached, the major impatiently ordered his men to lift the coffin out of the grave.

As they started to excavate around the box, Victor strode over. "What in the world is going on?"

"Save your breath, Herr Mayor," Keller snapped. "Your huffing and puffing will make no difference."

"This is sacred ground," Victor thundered.

"Then perhaps you can explain why you have dug it up so recently. Don't try to deny it."

Victor took a deep breath to steady his nerves. "Yes, we dug it up."

"You admit it?" Keller asked with barely concealed glee.

"Absolutely. And by all means let your men open up the box. But I would stand well clear when they do."

Keller hesitated. "Why?"

"The reason we dug it up was because we were so advised by the local minister for public interment. We were told we had to bury the body a couple of meters lower."

"And why would that be?"

"So the corpse didn't leak into the ground." Victor smiled triumphantly. "You see, the person inside this box didn't die in his sleep. He was poisoned by his brother-in-law to steal his inheritance. The arsenic still present in his body is enough to kill twenty men, we've been told. But if you don't believe me, feel free to bring the coffin up. Just beware of the fumes."

One or two of Keller's men had understood a smattering of what Victor had said and were now backing away warily. It was all I could do not to burst out laughing. Victor had called the major's bluff magnificently.

The muscles in Keller's jaw tightened as his eyes searched Victor's, then mine, for the truth. My mouth went dry as I waited for the outcome. Would he buy it?

After what seemed an age, a hollow smile spread across his face.

"Perhaps, after all, we should let the dead sleep a little longer," he muttered, before snapping out a series of orders to his men. They began hurriedly refilling the grave—a lot faster than they had dug it. Meanwhile the major leaped back into his car and returned to the manor house to avoid any further public humiliation.

That night, Keller left his troops playing cards and decided to pay another visit to Victor's bar. I was sitting with my father at our usual table while Victor and Benoît entertained us with old ballads.

As Keller took his seat, we shared an uneasy glance. Dominique, who was leaning against the bar, clapping in time to the music, took a deep breath before heading over to serve him. She stood mutely by his table, waiting for his order.

"Beer," Keller replied a little abruptly, before remembering himself. *"Bitte."*

Dominique nodded and turned to go.

"The village is in fine spirits tonight," he observed. "Maybe you think you have seen the back of me. . . ."

As he spoke, he studied Dominique closely, gauging her reaction. She blinked slowly before giving him a practiced smile. It was the kind she must have given a million times at Victor's stuffy municipal dinners.

"Your men have showered us with presents and food," she told him. "Why would we be pleased to see you go?"

Keller clearly suspected she was lying—was probably poking fun at him about the incident in the graveyard—but her performance was flawless. After a moment he returned her smile mechanically and she headed back to the bar.

Keller now turned his attention to the musicians. Benoît was playing his serpent, Victor his accordion. Even Félix had a mandolin, his square, callused fingers plucking away remarkably tenderly.

But as he looked closer, Keller's eye came to rest on an unused piano behind them. Curious, he stood up and wandered over.

Benoît's playing immediately became less assured as his eyes followed the highly polished jackboots squeaking across the floorboards. As usual, Félix showed no emotion whatsoever.

Keller waited patiently till they had finished their song, then clapped vigorously. "Bravo," he cheered, full of false bonhomie.

Victor smiled coolly and began to pack away his accordion.

"Don't tell me you are finishing already?" the major protested, pretending to look hurt. "I've only just got here."

"I need to change one of the barrels," Victor explained.

Keller nodded his understanding and, while Victor went behind the bar, he sauntered over to the piano. "Tell me. Why does no one play this?"

Victor gave my father a cautious glance. "That old thing? It's out of tune."

"Mind if I have a go?" Keller asked lightly.

I felt a twinge of panic. A bead of sweat formed on Victor's top lip as the major lifted the lid to look at the keyboard.

"Strange," he mused, glancing at the keys. "It looks in perfectly good condition."

By now, everyone in the bar was watching intently. Keller pulled back the stool and sat down, spreading his fingers across the keys in anticipation. After a moment he began to play.

To our surprise, the tune was sweet and lyrical, almost yearning. I could feel myself being drawn under its hypnotic spell.

Then, as abruptly as he had started, Keller stopped. "You lied to me," he said, raising an eyebrow speculatively at Victor. "The piano is perfectly in tune. So why say it wasn't?"

For a moment Victor was speechless; then Dominique came to his aid.

"Because of me."

Keller's eyes flicked to her, surprised. "Because of you?"

"Yes," she confirmed. "The piano was a present from my father. He cheated on my mother and now I can't bear to hear anyone play it. Victor was trying to protect me."

Keller's eyes narrowed as he weighed up her story. "I'm very sorry to hear that," he said eventually. "If your mother was half as beautiful as you, your father was a foolish man. I wonder, though, if I might take a look inside?"

I closed my eyes, waiting for the inevitable. Keller was on to us, I was certain of it. Even the stony expression on Félix's face was betraying a glimmer of fear. I saw one of his huge, muscular fists slowly clench into a fist.

"Inside? Whatever for?" Victor murmured.

"I am fascinated by pianos. I'd love to see how this one is strung. Do you mind?"

"Only if you promise to play us another tune," my father suddenly piped up.

"Alas, that is the only one my mother taught me," Keller replied, his lips curling into a smile.

"Shame," Papa sighed. "You have real talent."

But Keller was already on his feet and lifting the lid on the top of the piano. With a roomful of eyes out on stalks, he peered inside.

Then, after a moment, he gently closed the lid again.

The piano was empty—except for the strings, of course.

"See anything interesting?" my father inquired innocently.

Keller was clearly seething at being thwarted again, but he knew better than to show it.

"On second thought," he said, giving Dominique a tight smile, "I'll leave that beer." He clicked his heels in salute and strode out of the bar.

Once he had gone, we sighed with relief.

Fortunately Keller had failed to notice the piano's rather unconventional foot pedals: three in a row . . . just like an accelerator, a clutch and a brake pedal. . . .

27 The Germans Pack Up

The following day my father and I were sitting outside the bar, enjoying some of Dominique's delicious truffles. She'd used the last of the extra chocolate rations Keller had bestowed on the village when he first arrived. By now it had become blindingly obvious that he was going to get zero cooperation—or should I say collaboration—so the extra rations had suddenly dried up.

I'd been toying with my dusted chocolate truffle for over an hour, picking around the edge in a desperate attempt to make it last as long as possible, when a truckload of Keller's men swept through the village. Keller himself followed behind, riding imperiously in the back of his staff car, with Engel hunched beside him.

"Now where are they going?" Victor groaned.

Camille listened carefully. The roar of the truck's engine suddenly died just round the corner, and her eyes widened with alarm. "Dad's workshop!" she hissed.

Within seconds I was chasing after her as we raced across the square.

Sure enough, Keller's men were in the process of filing into her stepfather's forge.

As his men began their search, Keller wandered through to the lock-up at the back. A large rusty padlock barred any further access. Félix was sitting quietly in the corner, sipping his early morning coffee.

"I assume you have a key for this?" Keller inquired.

If Félix was alarmed, he wasn't showing it. In his usual unflappable manner, he carefully set down his coffee cup and began methodically working his way through a large bunch of keys till he found a small rusty one. He turned it in the lock and, after a good deal of fiddling, it creaked open. He tugged an old light cord and a filthy bulb flickered into life.

Keller took a step forward, his eyes adjusting to the gloom. The lock-up was crammed from floor to ceiling with all the old odds and ends we had raided all those months ago.

"Herr Engel, in your humble opinion, could any of these form part of the car we are looking for?"

The frail little man edged forward until he could scan the Aladdin's cave in front of him. I saw the tiny black pupils of his eyes swell to the size of saucers as he gazed from gearstick to steering wheel to fan belt.

"Well?" Keller prompted him.

"If you're asking me whether some of these parts could

be used in the assembly of a prototype vehicle, my answer would have to be y-yes," he stammered.

Keller's back stiffened, and Camille threw a jittery glance at her stepfather. Was the game finally up?

Félix, however, looked straight ahead, giving nothing away. Keller was about to bark an order to his sergeant when Engel cleared his throat again.

"However," he went on, "if you are asking whether, in my opinion, these really are the parts from the prototype we are looking for, I would conclusively say no."

For the second time in as many days, I saw the major's jaw tighten with irritation.

"May I ask why?"

Engel lifted up a large rusty suspension spring. "As far as I can tell, most of these parts are from a German reconnaissance airplane, circa 1917."

It was all Camille could do to stifle a snigger, but Major Keller took the information in his stride.

"A souvenir from the last war, it would seem," he said, smiling coldly at Félix. Without another word, he tugged on his leather gloves and strode back out toward his staff car. Engel nodded courteously to Félix, and then to each of us, before scurrying after him. Seconds later, the two of them disappeared in a cloud of dust.

As the remaining soldiers began to file out, Camille slipped a hand into her stepfather's. He turned and winked at us, then closed the doors and carefully relocked the padlock.

It was a narrow escape.

Later that afternoon, I was wandering back up the hill on my way home for dinner when I stopped dead in my tracks. Keller's troops were packing away their equipment and tents.

I felt a sudden surge of optimism. Were they going already?

I raced into the courtyard to check, and was about to head into the house when something caught my eye. The door to the old garage was slightly ajar.

Inside, Engel was studying the rusty remains of the old ambulance. It was the first thing the Germans had discovered when they'd started searching, but it had quickly been dismissed as a dinosaur. So what was Engel doing snooping around it again?

Seeing me, he sprang upright with a start, fumbling with his glasses. "I—I hope you don't mind," he stammered. "I couldn't resist another glance at it before we left."

"So it's true you're leaving?" I asked.

"Before nightfall, Major Keller assures me. Funny"— Engel gave me a shy smile—"I've become quite fond of this little village during our short stay."

Suddenly the door swung open and my father appeared. He was out of breath and looked unusually flustered. His eyes darted first to the ambulance, and then to the engineer. "Something I can help you with?" he demanded.

Engel smiled respectfully. "I was just explaining to Angelo that we are leaving. In a few hours or so."

"Well, we mustn't detain you," Papa answered rather shortly. He seemed unduly anxious to get Engel out of the garage as quickly as possible.

The little man nodded and shuffled toward the door.

But before he left he paused, his attention drawn back to the ambulance. "She must once have been a beautiful machine," he mused, almost in a reverie.

"A rust bucket, more like," my father grunted.

"Perhaps . . . Nonetheless, her suspension is highly original."

As he said the words, I spun round to look at the ambulance, confused. What did he mean the suspension was highly original? Surely it was just the rusty axle from the original chassis . . . ?

Then, all at once, the reality hit me like a freight train.

It wasn't the original. Or rather, bits of it were—the bonnet, the doors, various bits of old bumpers and canopies. But not the chassis. In fact, not the wheels, the engine, the seats—and especially not the suspension.

As I peered closer, I realized with horror that I was looking at the last prototype of the Tin Snail—or at least a skeleton of it. It had been crudely disguised with bits of rusty paneling to look like the ambulance.

How could this be? Every one of the prototypes had been broken up and buried. Unless . . .

I turned to glare at my father, who was now avoiding my eyes. It couldn't have been a clearer admission of guilt.

I reeled as the truth finally dawned. My own father, unable to bear the sight of all the precious prototypes being broken up and destroyed forever, had secretly hidden one right here, under our very noses, hoping it wouldn't be discovered.

Except that now it had. And what's more, by the very person we had been trying to conceal it from—Engel!

How could Papa have been so stupid!

There was a terrible silence as I looked daggers at him, but it was Engel who spoke first.

"Of course, it must have been designed specifically to carry casualties across the fields—to cushion the ride."

My father stared at him, obviously trying to work out how much he'd twigged. Did Engel suspect that this was the prototype in disguise? And if so, was he going to sound the alarm?

For a moment the two designers—one Italian but working for the French, the other German, but united by their passion for cars—held each other's gaze. I looked frantically from one to the other, trying desperately to work out how much Engel knew. If my heart had been racing before, I could now feel it thumping away in my chest. Surely he had guessed. . . .

"I hope that one day our paths will cross again, Signor Fabrizzi," Engel said with a smile. "When the war between our countries is well and truly in the past." Then he tipped his hat to each of us in salute and headed away.

I was stupefied. Could it be that he suspected nothing after all? Or—even harder to comprehend—was he turning a blind eye?

As his steps receded across the gravel, I let out a gasp. "He knows!"

Papa shushed me urgently. "Even if he does, I don't think he's going to say anything."

"But why? It doesn't make any sense!"

"Because I suspect that Herr Engel despises the Nazis every bit as much as we do," my father whispered. "Either way, I'm not about to start arguing with him." He headed for the door, but I wasn't finished with him yet. Not by a long shot.

"You lied to me. You promised you'd destroyed it," I hissed accusingly. I had never felt so angry or betrayed.

My father hung his head. "I'm sorry," he muttered. "I thought if I removed the bodywork and camouflaged it as the ambulance, they would never guess."

My head was still spinning with the shock of his treachery. "But that night—Christian said you were burying the parts all over the forest. Did he lie to me as well?"

"No," he insisted. "Christian helped me get the car to the garage and strip it down. But I could see that he was anxious to get home to his mother, so I sent him away."

"So no one would know about your deceit!" I spat the words out with disgust.

"I swear I was planning to break everything up," Papa protested. "But when I came to the chassis and suspension, I just couldn't do it." He looked into my eyes, ashamed. "I never meant to deceive you. But all I could think about was how much this car meant to us—to you. To see it destroyed for good . . . it was unthinkable."

"So you'd rather it fell into Keller's hands?" I snapped.

"Of course not!" he exclaimed. "I never thought they'd come—and even if they did, who would have suspected a beaten-up old ambulance sitting in full view?"

It was true—my father's ploy had managed to hoodwink Keller—but I wasn't about to forgive him that easily.

"I know I've been a stupid, irresponsible fool," he sighed, his eyes brimming with tears. "But if something had happened to me, or to Christian, the car would have been lost forever. Surely nothing could be worse than that—even the Germans finding it."

"You're wrong," I said, hearing my voice catch with emotion. "Don't you see? These people—Benoît, Victor, Camille—every one of them has put their life on the line to protect this car. They believed in us—and for what? So you could betray them." As my words sank in, my father looked down at the floor, ashamed. "Philippe was right," I muttered gloomily. "We are traitors."

I was about to walk out of the garage when suddenly Camille burst in, looking distraught.

"What is it?" I asked, alarmed. Had she heard what we'd been saying?

"Benoît," she said urgently. "The German officer is going to shoot him if he doesn't tell him where the car is hidden."

My father and I threw each other a look of horror. The next second we were sprinting out of the garage as fast as our legs would carry us.

28 A Terrible Choice

By the time we reached the village, a group of soldiers had dragged Benoît out of his house into the middle of the square. Major Keller was sitting at a table outside the bar tabac, sipping coffee as if nothing unusual was occurring. Meanwhile, Marguerite, sobbing uncontrollably, was fighting to get to her husband. It took three soldiers to restrain her—including, I noticed, the pimply youth who had been humiliated by her.

"What is the meaning of this?" my father demanded as he strode over to Keller.

The major glanced up and smiled cordially. "Ah, Signor Fabrizzi. Just in time. I am offering the monsieur a deal: to tell me where the prototype for your little car is hidden or to forfeit his life."

Suddenly there was a commotion. Victor had returned from an official meeting with the local council, but his way into the square was being barred.

"I insist you let me through this instant!" he yelled.

Keller waved to his soldiers and they stepped aside to let the plump mayor through.

"What on earth is going on?" Victor thundered as he approached.

Marguerite finally managed to push her way forward. "They're going to kill him!" she cried.

Victor's eyes bulged with shock.

"Strictly speaking, incorrect," Keller noted, after taking a sip of coffee. "I have simply given him the option of choosing that which he holds more dear: his life or the whereabouts of the car."

"This is an outrage," Victor protested. "You cannot do this!"

"On the contrary, Monsieur le Maire. I already am."

So many thoughts were racing through my head, I thought it would burst. I threw a panicked look to my father, but before he could react, another figure appeared in the square: Herr Engel. He glanced around in amazement, then shuffled over to Keller.

"Major, I must protest—"

But Keller cut him off midsentence. "My orders are to find the car—at any cost."

"But surely not like this—"

"You should be glad," Keller responded, a cruel glint in his eye. "Your bosses will probably promote you after this."

Suddenly a croaky voice interrupted them. It was Benoît.

"I have your answer, Major."

I shot another terrified look at my father as Keller stood up and approached the farmer.

"I'm glad you have decided to cooperate." The major smiled. "Well?"

"I—I should have told you before," Benoît stuttered guiltily.

"No matter. I am a forgiving man."

"Him . . . ," Benoît muttered darkly, throwing a look toward my father. My blood turned to ice.

"Go on," Keller encouraged him.

Benoît cleared his throat before continuing. "He took the engine out of his motorbike—the German one."

I closed my eyes in despair. Everything was surely lost now. But my father remained perfectly still, showing no emotion.

"And . . . ?" Keller urged the old man impatiently. "Where did he put it?"

Benoît took a deep breath and cast his eyes down toward his dusty shoes. "In my tractor."

The major looked startled. Clearly it wasn't the answer he was expecting. "In your tractor?" he asked, incredulous.

I opened my eyes, confused. What was the old man wittering on about?

"When the old engine died. He said it would work better, but he was a liar. It lasted about a day. It's my tractor you're looking for—but it's not exactly a car."

My father was staring straight at Benoît. Marguerite was also staring at him, unable to breathe. What madness was this?

Keller nodded sagely before slowly unbuttoning the leather flap of his holster and removing the Walther P38.

Marguerite started in horror. "Please . . . no, I beg you!"

My eyes widened in disbelief. I grabbed at my father's shirtsleeve. "Papa—you have to do something!"

"I commend you for your bravery, monsieur," Keller said to the old farmer. "If only your fellow countrymen had shown half your stubbornness, perhaps my soldiers and I would not be standing here now. But you're a fool to think you can lie to me." With that he brought his pistol level with Benoît's temple, the cold steel of the barrel pressing against the wisps of silver hair.

"Wait!" a voice suddenly boomed out across the square.

All eyes darted toward a tall, willowy figure in a gray rain-coat and crumpled trilby.

Bertrand.

"Monsieur Hipaux." Keller gave a sly smile. "I wondered that we had not seen you earlier."

Bertrand stared at him coldly. It was clear that he had nothing but loathing for him. "We both know perfectly well that your senior officers have been forcing me to manufac-ture lorries for your war effort."

"Lorries, I believe, that have a reputation for breaking down," the major noted caustically.

Bertrand gave him a hollow smile. "You can always allow us to return to building cars."

Major Keller didn't deign to answer this. "Time is against us, Monsieur Hipaux. Was there something you wished to say?"

Bertrand glanced across at Engel, who was standing

nearby. "Herr Engel knows only too well that for the last year or more we have been developing a car for the ordinary French worker. The reason you have not found it, and why none of these people will be able to show you its whereabouts, is that I ordered it to be destroyed."

Keller raised a skeptical eyebrow. "You're asking me to believe you simply destroyed a year's work?"

"Exactly that," Bertrand replied evenly.

"I'm sorry, but I don't believe you."

"You can kill as many people as you want." Bertrand shrugged. "Search as many pigsties as you can find, but you will not discover one trace of the car we tried to design. Believe me, we were very thorough." He turned to Engel again; the little man wore a look of complete astonishment.

"Forgive me, Herr Engel, but the idea of our little French car falling into the hands of a rival company, let alone the German military, was, well . . . unthinkable."

"As, indeed, it would be the other way round," Engel replied graciously. The two men exchanged a nod of understanding.

"So you are saying that nothing whatsoever of the car exists?" Keller asked doubtfully.

"There is something," Bertrand offered. He brought one of his long, gnarled fingers up to his temple and tapped it twice. "Up here."

The major studied him shrewdly, sensing he was being made a fool of in front of the entire village. "Then I suggest you accompany us back to Paris, where we can see if we can persuade you to share your memories with us in a little more detail," he said with more than a hint of cruel pleasure.

"Until then, unless I am given the whereabouts of the car in the next three hours, your friend the farmer here will still pay with his life."

"No!" Marguerite screamed, heartbroken.

"Major Keller!" Engel protested. "This is monstrous!"

Bertrand's face, never animated at the best of times, was now as gray as his overcoat as he tried to comprehend what he was hearing.

I too was speechless. Keller clearly believed that Bertrand was tricking him. The trouble was, he had been completely honest. As far as he was aware, all the prototypes had been destroyed and scattered to the four winds. Only my father and I knew the real truth.

I threw a look at Papa. Unless he confessed to keeping the car hidden in the barn—unless he gave up the secret the entire village had concealed for so long—Benoît would die.

I grabbed his arm, tears welling up in my eyes. "Tell them," I whispered hoarsely.

By now the major was settling into the back of his Mercedes.

"Major Keller," my father finally called out. He failed to hear over the noise of the car engine, so my father shouted his name louder.

This time he turned and barked something to his driver and the engine was switched off.

Suddenly all eyes were turned on my father. Bertrand too was watching him closely, sensing that something momentous was afoot.

"Let Benoît go," my father said, nodding toward the farmer.

"And why would I do that?" Keller asked, intrigued.

"Because I know where you can find what you are look-ing for."

Bertrand's face clouded. "What are you talking about? You know everything was destroyed."

He saw my father's black, soulful eyes looking back at him guiltily, and suddenly he understood.

He gasped in shock. "You kept something, didn't you?"

My father couldn't bear to look at him any longer and turned back to the major. "I can show you where we hid the parts," he told him grimly.

"No!" This time the voice came from Philippe, who had suddenly pushed his way through the crowd. "You mustn't tell them."

Victor spun round angrily. "Be quiet, Philippe!"

But he refused to listen. "Don't do this, I beg you," he urged my father.

"It's too late," Papa sighed.

"Perhaps you would prefer to die in the place of old Be-noît here?" Keller asked.

"If I have to," Philippe told him defiantly.

Victor stepped forward and grabbed his son roughly. "Philippe, enough!"

But Philippe shoved him away, his eyes now blazing with anger as he stared at my father. "If you give them this, then they have taken everything from us. We have already lost our country. Do not take what little pride we have left."

"Philippe, please!" Dominique was weeping.

"You would really rather die?" the major asked, fascinated.

Philippe turned to him slowly. "Gladly. Otherwise I have nothing left to live for. . . ."

"In that case, I'm afraid you are going to be bitterly disappointed," Keller said, smirking. "Because Signor Fabrizzi has already agreed to cooperate." He turned to my father. "Just like your fellow countrymen, it seems, you have seen sense and joined the winning side."

He gestured to his car, but my father pointedly ignored him. Instead, he turned to his mentor, Bertrand, who looked broken and defeated.

"I'm so sorry," he muttered.

Bertrand said nothing; simply turned and began to trudge back to his manor house. After a moment my father set out gloomily after him.

Keller shouted some further instructions to his men, then sank back into his seat as his car swept out of the square.

As the dust settled, I suddenly remembered Camille. When we'd first arrived in the square, I'd been vaguely aware of her standing nearby. Now, mysteriously, she was nowhere to be seen.

I was looking around to see if I could find her, when my eyes fell on Philippe, standing across the square from me. As we stared at each other, for the first time a small flicker of something like solidarity passed between us. Then I turned and hurried after my father.

29 The Tin Snail Rides Again!

As I reached the courtyard, I heard raised voices. Bertrand, Keller, Engel and my father were all gathered by the open door of the garage.

When I joined them, I immediately saw the reason for the heated debate. The ambulance—or rather, the Tin Snail—had gone.

"Congratulations, Signor Fabrizzi," Keller snarled. "All you have achieved with this futile exercise is to waste fifteen minutes of your own time."

Like me, my father was completely at a loss. "This is no trick," he assured Bertrand. "It was here."

"Then may I suggest that you find it," said the major. "If I'm right, it wasn't designed for speed, so it shouldn't have gone far," he added sarcastically.

I edged out of the garage, my mind whirring. No one apart from me and my father knew about the secret prototype being hidden here—so who would have known to take it? Then, all at once, I remembered how Camille had been outside when I was talking to my father earlier.

Of course! Camille. Why hadn't I realized it? She had disappeared from the square soon after Bertrand had appeared. And as one of the pioneering test dummies, she would at least have some idea how to drive the disguised ambulance. But where could she be? Suddenly a thought leaped into my head.

Minutes later, having sneaked unnoticed out of the courtyard, I was tearing up the hillside at the back of the house. I was soon hidden among the trees, but there was no time to slow down. I raced on, gasping for breath as my lungs burned.

I ran as hard as I could until I emerged from the woodland onto the potholed lane near the racetrack. Then I dived into the woods on the other side and down the hill toward the river where Camille, Dominique and I had spent those precious few weeks swimming.

At last I reached the riverbank. Down below, the black stream chattered its way over the rocks.

Finally I saw what I was looking for: the old water mill. There, on the edge of the steep embankment, where the wooden beam jutted out above the river, stood the ambulance. Camille was standing beside it.

I raced down to her. "What are you doing here?" I cried.

Camille rushed to the back of the car and began to lean her shoulder against it, pushing with all her might.

"Help me!" she shouted. "I'm going to hide it in the water."

"We can't," I protested. "If we destroy it, what will happen to Benoît?"

"You and your father and I are the only ones who know about the car," she said. "If we hide it in the water, it can stay that way. Now help me!"

I hesitated for a moment, then realized that she was right. I threw my weight into trying to heave the car forward, but the grassy mound leading up to beam was in the way. The car refused to budge more than a few inches.

"It's no use," I huffed. "It's too steep."

Camille cried out in frustration. Suddenly my head jerked to the side: I'd heard something. I hushed Camille and she fell silent, straining to listen. The noise came again—this time clearer.

"Dogs," I hissed. "It's Keller's men. They must have followed me."

Camille's eyes were wide with panic. "We can't let them take it."

Suddenly I had an idea. "We can drive it to your father's forge and melt it down."

"There isn't time," she protested, but I was already ahead of her.

"The most important thing is to destroy the suspension. The rest they can have."

"But how are we going to drive through a village full of Nazi storm troopers?"

Suddenly we caught a glimpse of gray tunic and steel helmet. It was now or never.

"Come on!" I shouted. I turned to clamber into the driver's seat, only to find Camille had beaten me to it.

"What are you doing?" I protested.

"You think I'm going to let you drive after last time?" she scoffed. There wasn't time to argue. I leaped into the passenger seat and she rammed the gearstick into reverse.

Farther along the riverbank, a German shout went up and several hounds were released. Spittle flying from their jaws, the animals tore their way through the undergrowth, gaining on us fast.

"Hurry, come on!" I screamed.

"I'm trying—it won't move!"

The wheels were spinning uselessly in the leaves. Suddenly a shot rang out. It fizzed through the leaves, snapping a branch just beside us.

"They're shooting at us!" I shouted.

At last the wheels dug into solid earth and the car shuddered into life.

The race was on!

Bullets pinged past us, clanking off the metalwork and thumping into tree trunks. I cowered behind the dashboard as Camille floored the accelerator.

Gathering momentum, the Tin Snail careered through the undergrowth. With a massive crash of splintering wood, we burst out of the trees, crunching down onto the rutted track ahead. The force of the impact crumpled the bonnet, shearing the bumper clean off.

"Go!" I cried. A shower of sparks flew up from the front axle as Camille swung the steering wheel round and the car nearly keeled over onto its side.

"Why can't this thing go any faster?" she screamed.

"It's not designed for speed, remember?" I shouted back over the noise of the engine as we bounced our way along the potholed track. I glanced over my shoulder to see if anyone was following us, but the road was clear. "I think we've lost them."

My words were cut short by Camille slamming on the brakes, sending my face thumping into the dashboard. Coming the other way, its tracks chewing up the fencing beside the road, was the tank.

I spun round and saw a plowed field to our right. "Quick! Through there."

"We won't be able to outrun it."

"This is the one thing it is designed for!"

"And that isn't?" Camille shouted back as the tank rumbled toward us, its barrel swiveling terrifyingly in our direction.

"Just do it!" I snapped.

Camille had no choice. She slammed her foot to the floor and yanked the wheel round. The car heaved itself over the edge of the road and onto the track. With every rut we hit, the bodywork rattled and shook where it had been hurriedly welded on by my father.

"It's not going to make it!" Camille cried.

"It has to!"

Behind us, the tank had come to a stop before swiveling toward us and lurching forward. Its enormous caterpillar tracks simply flattened every rut it went over.

Inside the Tin Snail, the metalwork was now groaning in protest.

"We're not going fast enough," Camille said despairingly. No sooner had she said it than a large section of the ambulance's paneling sheared off and sank into the mud behind us. Freed from the excess weight, the car surged forward with renewed vigor.

"We have to get rid of the other panels," I yelled over the cacophony.

"I'm kind of busy here!" Camille shouted back, desperately trying to navigate her way across the field. I leaned back and put both feet across her lap.

"What are you doing?" she shrieked, confused.

By way of an answer, I kicked hard against the door next to her. After three or four heavy blows, it flew clean off its hinges. I now turned my attention to the back panel. With each piece of bodywork that flew off, the car gained momentum.

By now the tank, which until a moment ago had been gaining ruthlessly on us, had begun to fall back.

The Tin Snail—reduced now to little more than an engine on wheels—was sailing across the field. If ever proof was needed of its revolutionary suspension, this was definitely it.

The track on the other side of the field loomed ahead, and Camille threw the car right and gunned the engine again. We only had to cross the river at the bottom of the hill, and then the village would be less than a hundred meters ahead of us. . . .

Suddenly Camille and I exclaimed at the same time: "The bridge!"

The only way across the river was the rickety old structure Christian's sports car had destroyed. As far as we knew, it had yet to be repaired. If it was still out of action, the race was as good as over—it would be only minutes before the tank caught up with us.

With nothing to lose, Camille accelerated down the track, which twisted on its final approach to the bridge. In a matter of seconds our fate would be sealed one way or another.

"Is the bridge there?" Camille yelled as she tried to turn the manually operated windscreen wiper to clear the screen.

"I don't know."

"Yes or no?"

"Yes!" I blurted, screwing my eyes up to peer ahead. As far as I could tell, there was a new section of wooden track stretching out across the water.

But as the bridge loomed up in front of us, we suddenly saw to our horror it was only half complete. Before we could do anything, the car crashed onto the wooden boards and took off.

For a hideous second I had visions of plunging into the water again. But, as luck would have it, Christian's sports car was still half-buried in the riverbed, reeds now growing up through its leather upholstery. The Tin Snail thumped down onto its bonnet, momentarily bottoming out. A force like that should have sheared the suspension rods in half—yet miraculously, with a wrench of splintering metalwork, we simply bounced off it and landed on the riverbank beyond.

Unbelievably, the car still carried on—mostly out of sheer forward momentum, but who cared? It was moving.

Back on the other side, the Panzer had attempted to

muscle its way straight across the half-formed bridge. But the moment its colossal weight hit the woodwork, the whole structure collapsed, and the tank slumped onto its side, its caterpillar tracks spinning forward and then backward, spraying up mud and stones.

No two ways about it: it was stuck fast.

Minutes later, the battered skeleton of the Tin Snail rattled its way up the track into the village, a hubcap sparking off the pavement and clattering against the wall. Camille tugged the wheel left and urged the tiny spluttering engine toward her father's forge on the opposite side of the square.

Our faces were covered in mud and weeds from the river, but we were elated. We had maybe two to three minutes to start sabotaging what was left of the car before Keller's men arrived. Anything now would feel like a victory, no matter how token.

Suddenly Camille screamed. In the middle of the road ahead of us stood the unmistakable figure of Keller. As we barreled across the square, straight toward him, he calmly raised his pistol and took aim. Camille and I dived for cover as he let off five rounds into the bonnet.

Riddled with bullet holes, the car veered dementedly toward him before crashing through several tables, and straight into Victor's bar. Destroying everything in its path, it thumped into the counter, its bonnet crumpling like tin foil as steam hissed out of its punctured radiator.

For a moment Camille and I were too dazed to move. Behind us, voices began to cry out in alarm and I spotted the blurred form of my father sprinting across the square. By now Victor and Dominique were also scrambling their way through the wreckage to reach us.

Through the door, I saw Keller return his pistol smoothly to its holster, a look of satisfaction on his face. Seconds later, two army trucks roared into the square, spilling out troops, but he held up a hand to stop them. "That will not be necessary," he told them calmly.

My father and Victor managed to drag us, battered and bruised, from the wreckage of the car. As Keller strode toward us, Papa lunged at him ferociously. For a moment he feared for his life—till several soldiers raced forward and roughly overpowered my father.

"You animal!" he railed. "You meant to kill them."

"Not at all," Keller assured him icily. "I'm a marksman. I meant merely to disable the car. Had I wished to shoot the children, believe me, they would already be dead."

By now Engel, Bertrand and Philippe had reached us, all ashen with shock.

"M-Major Keller," Engel stammered, incensed, "I shall be lodging an official complaint about your behavior with the German minister himself. Your conduct is nothing short of barbaric, and you bring disgrace on yourself and Germany."

Keller listened impassively. "Complain all you want, but I have carried out my orders—not to mention yours. As you see," he said, nodding toward the wrecked car, lodged nose-first in the bar, "I have found your prototype."

As his men set about salvaging what was left of the car and loading it onto the truck, I slumped, defeated, on the curb. Moments later my father joined me.

"We failed," I said dejectedly, suddenly understanding the futility of everything we'd tried to do.

"No," he sighed. "I was the one who let you down. If I'd just done what Bertrand said . . ."

"I—I thought the car would change everything," I stammered, my voice catching with emotion.

"How do you know it won't?"

"I mean now," I protested. "Between you and Maman."

My father lifted my chin, gently smoothing away my tears. "What is it Bertrand used to say? Some things aren't meant to be. . . ."

"The rest aren't meant to be yet," I added.

My father smiled at me wistfully. "Maybe," he said. "Maybe."

30　An Unscheduled Stop at the Train Station

And that would have been the end of the story. The prototype would have been sent back to Germany and lost to France forever—had it not been for Benoît's plan.

It turned out that a number of the local wine growers had grown sick of the invading Germans looting their cellars and shipping their finest wines to Germany. To get their own back, a select few of Benoît's friends had begun a series of daring midnight raids on the German freight trains. No sooner had each barrel of wine been loaded up to begin its journey north to Germany than the local stationmaster would tip off the farmers. They would then intercept the train, sometimes before it had even left the station, and secretly empty the barrels, replacing the wine with water.

Two nights after the dreadful day when Keller found the

car, a friend of Benoît's from a nearby vineyard arrived at Victor's bar and whispered an interesting piece of information into his ear. The stationmaster had told him about another consignment heading back to Germany. Only this time it wasn't wine, but assorted parts of the Tin Snail itself.

The wrecked remains of the chassis, engine and, most importantly, suspension had been duly numbered, logged and then packed into crates by Keller's men to be taken back to Germany the following night.

Major Keller had overseen the operation himself and watched as the precious cargo was loaded onto the trucks, bound for the main station on the outskirts of Boutonne. He then pulled on his leather gloves, slid down his goggles and sat back in his staff car as it swept out of the town, never to return.

But no sooner had Keller's entourage thundered away than Camille, my father, Victor, Benoît, Félix, Philippe and I sprang into action. Even Marguerite came along for the ride.

Taking Benoît's tractor and various carts drawn by horses and a remarkably revitalized Geneviève, we set off for the station at nightfall.

There, shortly after midnight, we stole across the tracks and hid behind the freight carriages.

Marguerite, meanwhile, approached the lone guard keeping watch in the signal box. Under her arm was a bottle of Benoît's strongest home brew. The guard didn't take much persuading to join her in a nightcap, but he hadn't reckoned on Marguerite's iron constitution.

While we crouched in the shadow of the freight train,

the guard finally passed out. As he began to snore like a warthog, Marguerite crept to the window and signaled the all clear. Immediately we sprang into action.

Following the information from the stationmaster, it didn't take me long to identify the carriage that contained the Tin Snail. I nodded to Félix, who produced a giant pair of bolt cutters.

Checking that the coast was clear, he crunched his way through the padlock and we slid the carriage door open. Once safely inside, we made short work of prizing open the carefully numbered crates, all emblazoned with a red-and-black Nazi swastika. Inside each one lay a precious component of the wrecked prototype, packed in straw for its journey back to Germany.

"Where do we start?" I hissed.

"How about with this?" Victor suggested, producing from under a blanket the section of wooden plow that had hung above the bar. He removed one of the pieces of the prototype and replaced it with the farm machinery.

And so it continued into the night. As each box was opened, the parts of the Tin Snail were lifted out and replaced with assorted fakes. Then, one by one, the crates, containing a hotchpotch of broken farming equipment and household ironmongery, were resealed.

It amused me to imagine the scene in Germany, days later, when, under the watchful gaze of Major Tobias Keller, the crates were reopened and a group of nonplussed technicians attempted to reassemble the Tin Snail. . . .

After the success of our midnight raid, news spread fast. Soon, a new spirit of defiance was sweeping the country.

The ordinary French people were beginning to realize that their German oppressors weren't so benevolent after all. In fact, they were systematically bleeding the country dry.

Food became very scarce. More alarming still, the Nazis were dragging away anyone who dared to speak out against them.

But the German occupiers had underestimated the will of the French people. Soon—spurred on by the story of the Tin Snail, I liked to think—the groups of peasants intercepting German trains were joined by others, until a whole secret army of fighters had sprung up all over the country.

The French Resistance, as it was soon called, would become a fearsome group of heroes who risked everything to sabotage the German war effort, and Philippe was among its most daring leaders.

EPILOGUE

The Paris Motor Show, 1948

It's a little before nine o'clock in the morning, and I can feel my stomach tightening into a knot as I wait for the doors of the Grand Palais to be thrown open for the Paris Motor Show.

I'm twenty-three now, and people say I've got my father's muscular build—which I think is a polite way of saying I have his square head. Others say I have the paler looks of my mother.

My father is sitting beside me, and judging by the way he keeps stirring sugar into his espresso, he's as nervous as I am.

The war and its aftermath have taken their toll on him, I realize. His face is more deeply lined, his mane of black hair a little thinner, with the first flecks of gray. A lot of his wild sorcerer's passion has vanished: it's now certain that he and my mother won't get back together after all.

At first I refused to believe it; I kept hoping that somehow they would be reunited. But it wasn't to be. Now I've come to accept that people aren't like cars. You can't always fix something that's broken.

It's eight years since we moved back to Paris. Soon after our raid on the freight train, my father and I returned to help Bertrand build trucks for the Germans. Some wondered how we could bring ourselves to collaborate like that—but little did they know what Bertrand was really up to. Not only was he able to keep employing his entire workforce; he was quietly and efficiently running a little underground sabotage movement of his own.

As Keller himself had noted, Bertrand's lorries had something of a reputation for breaking down at the most inconvenient moments. What Keller had never figured out, however, was why.

Bertrand had secretly instructed us to put the notch on the oil dipstick a centimeter lower than it should be. A tiny adjustment that would be lost on the untrained eye, but would mean that every engine ran out of oil unexpectedly, often with catastrophic effects.

Eventually, four years later, the war came to an end. As the defeated Germans fled back across the border, they left a trail of destruction behind them. Revenge was swift, and soon anyone suspected of collaborating with the invaders was arrested and put on trial. Senior German officers and officials were also being rounded up—among them two whom my father and I knew only too well.

One, predictably, was Major Keller. The other was Dr. Ferdinand Porsche, who was to spend the next two years in a French prison. Production of his own people's car was halted—for the moment, at least.

All of which meant that another car was now fighting to take the crown at the 1948 Paris Motor Show.

Since those first corrugated-iron prototypes we'd tested out in Benoît's field, the Tin Snail has been through some major changes. The bodywork has been restyled, some of its sharper edges smoothed out, its engine improved.

But there's one thing Bertrand insists will never change: the Tin Snail is a no-frills car. It's a working animal, not a luxury Thoroughbred. For that reason, he has declared that there will be a strict waiting list. Only those who can prove they're working artisans—the hardworking farmers and bakers for whom the car was designed—can buy one.

Now, having added several more spoonfuls of sugar to my own espresso, I join my father to watch the people as they start to stream into the Grand Palais. Already they are beginning to gather around the car—though it's hard to tell if their confusion is because they think it's beautiful or plain daft.

"It's a good sign," I suggest optimistically. "At least they've noticed it."

"They'll hate it," my father groans. "Just like the newspapers."

It's true. Journalists have already taken against the car.

They're used to cars being elegant, stylish. But the Tin Snail, perched up on its plinth, is most definitely and unashamedly no such thing.

There's no point denying it: it's, well, basic; a backstreet kid fighting dirty.

Bertrand, amazingly, is taking all this in his stride. I know that he was expecting a backlash from the papers, but nothing like this. The press are openly laughing, jeering at the "ugly duckling," as they're calling it: another disaster for Hipaux, their headlines are crowing.

Down below me, his secretary, Madame Detrice, is clucking around a cluster of young assistants. Their job is to check every potential buyer to see if they qualify. If their job is too middle-class, or if they earn too much, they're simply turned away.

The press are guffawing. With such a financial disaster on his hands, surely Bertrand is insane to think he can turn away paying customers!

I cast around and pick out Bertrand himself, busy fielding questions from the press. Suddenly a familiar hand gently touches his arm. Even after all these years, I recognize him immediately.

Engel.

"I have come to congratulate you on your success," I overhear him say, smiling in his customary guarded manner.

"I don't know about that. Most of this lot hate it," Bertrand replies, throwing a rueful look at the throng of journalists.

"They don't matter," Engel assures him. He turns and

nods toward the people forming an orderly line behind Madame Detrice. "These are the ones who are voting with their feet."

As Bertrand turns, I follow his gaze. To my astonishment, a large queue has steadily been gathering behind our backs. With every passing second, more and more people are now joining it. Ordinary, common workers, wearing their best Sunday suits, are patiently waiting to fill in application forms.

"Papa." I tug at my father's arm. "Look."

Reluctantly he glances round. For a moment his eyes don't focus. Then he sees it.

The queue of prospective buyers is already snaking across the great hall. In a matter of minutes it will stretch outside and into the street.

Very gradually, by word of mouth, a legend is being born. Despite the best attempts of the press to derail it, the French public are taking the ugly little car to their hearts. In fact, astonishingly, some of them don't even think it's ugly at all!

Bertrand's faith in my father has been utterly vindicated. The Tin Snail is nothing short of a miracle.

Suddenly a figure in the crowd catches my eye. It is the merest glimpse, but I'm certain.

Camille!

I leap to my feet and begin to push my way forward. It's no easy task—the crowd is now twenty or more deep, pressing around the stand. With every step, I feel my chest tightening, but I don't care. I have to see if it's really her.

I fight my way through to the other side of the hall, only to find no sign of her. Searching the crowd desperately, I feel my world darken again. Did I just imagine her after all? Crushed, I turn to go back to my father when I notice that the driver's door of the Tin Snail is slightly open.

My heart stops and I begin to edge forward. Slipping under the rope cordoning off the stand, I step up onto the plinth and cautiously approach the passenger window. No one seems to have noticed me: Bertrand is too busy fending off the press, while Madame Detrice and her girls are inundated with inquiries.

As I edge toward the car, I feel as if I've gone back ten years to that fateful day when I drove the display model clean off the stand.

I reach for the door handle and ease it open.

Camille is sitting in the driver's seat; she turns toward me casually. "You didn't fix the windscreen wiper, then."

"Nope," I concede before climbing in beside her.

For a moment we sit in silence—till Camille can clearly bear it no longer.

"You stopped writing," she says accusingly.

"Can you blame me? I heard you got married."

"No—I got engaged," she corrects me.

I steal a glance at her finger. There's no ring.

"People get unengaged, stupid," she says scornfully.

Suddenly my heart is beating like a drum and my mouth has gone dry. My hand instinctively begins scratching the back of my neck.

"So why are you here? To buy one of these?" I ask as casually as I can.

"Don't need one."

"Why . . . ?"

"Because I'm moving to Paris," she announces matter-of-factly.

My heart is thumping so loudly, I'm convinced she can hear it. "Oh, yes? Anywhere nice?" I ask.

"I haven't seen the apartment yet. I was hoping you'd help me find it."

I stare at her, and she returns my gaze without blinking.

"Are you going to do that all day?" she asks eventually.

"Do what?"

"Stare at me."

A thousand different hopes and thoughts crowd into my mind at once.

"Where are the keys for this thing, anyway?" she asks impatiently. "I want to see how she handles."

"Take it from me—this isn't the best place for a test-drive."

"Well, in that case, you'd better take me for a spin some other day," she says, then slowly sinks down in her seat. I follow her lead, hunkering down beside her, till we're both out of sight of the crowds.

She turns to me, her face now only inches from mine. There's that same old mischievous glint in the corner of her eye. "Well . . . ?"

"Well, what?"

"Go on, then."

"Go on what?" I ask, baffled.

She sighs, exasperated, then grabs hold of the lapels of

my jacket and tugs me closer. The sudden shift in balance makes the car lurch unexpectedly to one side.

"You're going to need to fix that flipping suspension," she says, scowling.

And then she kisses me.

The True Story Behind *The Tin Snail*

On a snowy winter's day in 1995, something very special was found hidden in a barn in the French countryside not far from Paris, something that had been kept a secret from the world for nearly fifty years. High up in the hayloft were three of the earliest prototypes for a car that had become a legend in France and around the world. It was called the Deux Chevaux—or 2CV for short.

When I saw the newspaper photograph of these cars being winched out of the barn, I was immediately fascinated by how they had come to be there. It turned out that, like the car Angelo helps create in my story, the original 2CV was designed to be a revolutionary new vehicle: a car for the ordinary French worker. When war broke out in September 1939, the head of Citroën really did order that all the prototypes be scrapped so that the German army—or rather the spies for Citroën's rivals—couldn't steal them. Two young engineers who had worked on the car, however, couldn't bear to see their precious designs destroyed and promptly took matters into their own hands. . . .

As I started to research the story, I wondered what would

have happened if the Germans had discovered these prototypes . . . and the tale of the Tin Snail was born.

A lot of my story is a work of imagination—there is no evidence that the German army ever made it to the village where the prototypes were hidden. But several of my key characters are inspired by the real inventors of the 2CV: in particular, Flaminio Bertoni, who really was Italian and drove an old BMW motorbike; and André Lefèbvre, a dashing engineer who really drank only champagne and drove rally cars.

Special mention must also go to the head of Citroën at that time, Pierre-Jules Boulanger, a very wise and courageous man without whom the 2CV (or Tin Snail) would almost definitely never have existed. It was his idea that the car had to be cheap and sturdy enough to drive over a plowed field without spilling any beer or breaking any eggs. What's more, he really did move the oil marks on dipsticks so that the cars he had to make for the German army always broke down!

The last 2CV was made in 1990, after which production stopped for good. But if you look hard enough, you can still see the odd lovingly cared-for model on the road. Thanks to its revolutionary suspension, however, you probably won't see it turning over as it comes round the bend. . . .

—Cameron McAllister

About the Author

Cameron McAllister is a TV scriptwriter and has worked on shows such as *Robinson Crusoe*, *Spooks Code 9*, *Primeval*, and *Emmerdale*. He grew up near the beaches of Cornwall, England, and now lives in Brighton with his wife, four sons, and Floss the dog.

About the Illustrator

Sam Usher's debut picture book, *Can You See Sassoon?*, was nominated for the Kate Greenaway Award and shortlisted for the Read It Again! Award, the Waterstones Children's Book Prize, and the Red House Book Award. Sam lives in North London with an eighty-eight-year-old housemate and spends his time playing the piano, trespassing, and drawing in his favorite café.